Special Delivery

McIntyre Security Bodyguard Series
Book 14

by

April Wilson

Copyright © 2021 April E. Barnswell/
Wilson Publishing LLC
All rights reserved.

Cover by Steamy Designs
Proofread by Amanda Cuff (Word of Advice)

Published by
April E. Barnswell
Wilson Publishing LLC
P.O. Box 292913
Dayton, OH 45429
www.aprilwilsonauthor.com

ISBN: 9798528408972

No part of this publication may be reproduced, stored in a retrieval system, copied, shared, or transmitted in any form or by any means without the prior written permission of the author. The only exception is brief quotations to be used in book reviews. Please don't steal e-books.

This novel is entirely a work of fiction. All places and locations are used fictitiously. The names of characters and places are figments of the author's imagination, and any resemblance to real people or real places is purely coincidental and unintended.

Books by April Wilson

McIntyre Security Bodyguard Series:

Vulnerable

Fearless

Shane (a novella)

Broken

Shattered

Imperfect

Ruined

Hostage

Redeemed

Marry Me (a novella)

Snowbound (a novella)

Regret

With This Ring (a novella)

Collateral Damage

Special Delivery

McIntyre Security Search and Rescue Series:

Search and Rescue

A Tyler Jamison Novel:

Somebody to Love

Somebody to Hold

A British Billionaire Romance:

Charmed (co-written with Laura Riley)

Audiobooks and Upcoming Releases:

For links to my audiobooks and upcoming releases, visit my website: www.aprilwilsonauthor.com

The McIntyres

- Bridget and Calum McIntyre, the parents
- Shane McIntyre and Beth Jamison-McIntyre, husband and wife, son Luke and new baby
- Sophie McIntyre and husband, Dominic Zaretti
- Jamie McIntyre and girlfriend, Molly Ferguson
- Jake McIntyre and wife, Annie, with son Aiden and twin daughters, Emerly and Everly
- Hannah McIntyre
- Lia McIntyre and fiancé, Jonah Locke
- Liam McIntyre (Lia's twin)

The Jamisons

- Ingrid Jamison (Beth and Tyler's mother)
- Tyler Jamison and boyfriend, Ian Alexander

Other Characters

- Sam Harrison, Beth's personal bodyguard
- Cooper, Shane's right-hand man & Sam's fiancé
- Killian Devereaux (works for Shane's security company)
- Mack Donovan (security) and girlfriend, Erin O'Connor (Beth's friend)
- Haley Donovan (Mack's teenage daughter)
- Miguel Rodriguez (security)
- Philip Underwood (security)
- Elly and George Peterson (caretakers of the Kenilworth estate)

1

Beth McIntyre

It's Thursday afternoon, and our penthouse apartment is quiet for a change. My sweet toddler, Luke, is taking his afternoon nap. My husband is at his downtown office tying up some loose ends before our new baby arrives and he goes on paternity leave. Our two housemates, Sam and Cooper, are nowhere to be seen. I suspect they're having some quality *alone time* in their private suite.

Which leaves me free to have some alone time of my own.

I fill the huge soaking tub in my bathroom with warm water—not too hot, of course, as I'm pregnant—and pour in some rose-scented bubble bath. I light the trio of candles sitting on the ledge between the tub and the window, and then I turn out the lights and lower the blinds so it's nice and cozy in here. The candlelight makes for a relaxing ambience. And right now, I could really use some quiet time. I've been nesting lately, getting everything ready for the arrival of our new baby—cleaning house, preparing the bassinet, washing our stash of newborn baby clothes, stocking diapers. Everything.

After slipping out of my robe, I step gingerly into the bath and sink into the soothing water, trying to be as graceful as I can at nine months pregnant. I'm actually two days past my due date. Our new baby will be here anytime.

As the water envelops me in its steamy warmth, I let out a heart-felt sigh and slip down into the water as low as I can so my chin is resting just above the waterline. I rest my head back on a thick towel and let the water work its magic on my aching muscles.

After chasing a toddler around all day, my back and feet are killing me. A few minutes of peace and quiet is exactly what I need. I just hope I can eke out a good half-hour soak before Luke wakes up hungry for his dinner. So far, according to the soft snoring sounds coming through the baby monitor perched on the bathroom counter, he's still sound asleep. He's just getting over a cold, and I can hear his steady, raspy breathing over the intercom.

I close my eyes and let my thoughts wander as the warm water laps against my belly and breasts. Cocooned in this soothing warmth, I lose all track of time.

"Please tell me you aren't actually asleep in a tub full of water."

My eyes flutter open at the sound of the low, somewhat-amused voice of my husband. I was so out of it, I didn't hear him come in. I gaze up at Shane, attempting to appear fully alert, when in truth, I was honestly close to dozing off. I smile guiltily. "I was just resting my eyes."

His smile tells me I'm not fooling him. "I find the idea of my wife falling asleep in the bathtub rather unnerving." He loosens his charcoal gray tie, his gaze sweeping my naked body. "Where is everyone?"

"Luke's napping, and the boys have disappeared."

He grins when I refer to our best friends as *the boys*. Cooper is in his fifties and Sam, who's in his late twenties, is older than I am. They're hardly boys.

Shane removes his Rolex and lays it on the bathroom counter, along with his phone and wallet. Then he starts unbuttoning his shirt, his movements slow and unhurried. "If you'd told me you were naked, I would have come home sooner."

As his long fingers release each of his shirt buttons, I feel a corresponding flutter between my legs, as if his fingers are *there*, touching me, teasing me. Suddenly, the bathroom air feels even warmer, and my skin heats.

One thing about being pregnant, it really messes with my hormones. It seems like I'm constantly in a state of arousal. Lately, I've been insatiable. And poor Shane worries so much about hurting me or the baby—which I tell him is impossible—he has a hard time relaxing and simply enjoying sex while we can still have it. I keep telling him there's nothing to worry about—it's not like we're hanging from the chandeliers.

We should make the best use of the time we have before the baby's born, because after that, we'll have to abstain from sex for a while.

After shrugging out of his shirt and dropping it to the floor, Shane removes his white undershirt and goes to work on his leather belt. As his long fingers work at the buckle, the tantalizing sensations between my legs intensify, making me squirm. A moan escapes me before I can stifle it, and Shane's expression heats as his gaze locks onto mine.

When I shift position, the water laps at my breasts, which are heavy and aching and so exquisitely sensitive right now.

Mesmerized, I watch him strip naked. His shoes and socks hit the floor, followed by his charcoal trousers, leaving him in just a pair of black boxer-briefs. My gaze sweeps over his body, from his bare feet, up his long legs, and to his hips. His erection strains against the soft cotton fabric of his briefs, and there's no mistaking what's on his mind as he drops his briefs to the floor.

My gaze skims the ridges of his abdomen, his broad chest, and shoulders. I want my hands on him. I want to feel those hard muscles and tendons as they flex.

His handsome face transforms with a slightly-crooked grin. His kissable lips are framed by a trim brown beard, and his electric-blue eyes are locked on me.

"Scoot," Shane says as he motions for me to move forward. He carefully slides in behind me, then pulls me back against his chest. His legs are on either side of my hips, his knees slightly bent, and I'm cradled between his strong thighs. I can feel his erection prodding me from behind, and it sends shivers down my spine.

His wet hands glide up on either side of me to frame my enormous baby bump. "How's our little girl today?"

I laugh softly. He's so sure we're having a girl. Secretly, I suspect he's right because this pregnancy is nothing like my first, but I'm not going to tell him that. It's more fun to tease him. "Or boy."

He grunts noncommittally. "Or boy. But I'm telling you, she's a girl."

"We'll know soon enough, won't we?"

"Mm-hmm," he murmurs, distracted as he presses his lips to my temple. He plants nibbling kisses down my cheek, down the side of my neck, then across one shoulder. His hands slide up to cup my breasts, and he teases my sensitive nipples with gentle thumbs.

Electricity shoots straight to my core, heating me up and making me flush with need. His touch makes me moan and squirm.

Shane draws lazy circles over my nipples, and we both watch my areolas pucker tightly. A groan escapes me, and I feel a desire to move, to rock my hips. When the need intensifies, I grab one of his hands and bring his fingers to the hot, throbbing spot between my legs. Without further prompting, he opens me up and slides a finger over my clit and down to my opening.

I moan loudly as he sucks on the side of my neck. "Shane, please."

"Are you sure?" he asks quietly. Unhurriedly. As if he has all the time in the world.

While I'm practically burning up inside. "God, yes."

When the tip of his finger eases inside me, I lean my head back against his shoulder and gasp. "Yes, please."

He proceeds to tease me, ramping up my desire to a fever pitch. His thumb on my clit, rubbing tiny circles, and his long slick finger inside me, stroking me—it's too much and yet not nearly enough. I need him, now, inside me.

I lean my head back and turn my face for a kiss. His lips latch onto mine, and he kisses me until I'm breathless, his tongue teasing mine.

"Shane, please," I say.

He steps out of the tub and dries off quickly with an oversized bath towel. Then he takes my hand and helps me out. He grabs a fresh towel and wipes me down while I stand naked before him. His gaze is hot and hungry as it sweeps every inch of my body, from my pussy to my big belly to my pregnancy-heavy breasts. I used to be so self-conscious when I was naked in front of him, but not anymore. A man can't fake that kind of reaction. His muscles are taut as his chest rises and falls with heavy breaths. His nostrils flare with arousal. Even if I feel self-conscious at times, I know he likes what he sees, and that's all that matters to me.

Standing behind me, he wraps his arms around me and settles his hands on my belly. The baby's doing somersaults at the moment, so we both stare in awe as my belly ripples with movement.

"A woman's body is a miraculous thing," he muses as he splays his hands over my undulating bump.

Carefully, he sweeps me up into his strong arms and carries me out of the bathroom and into our bedroom, heading straight for the king-size bed that is the main focal point of our room. He sets me on the floor so he can pull the bedding to the foot of the bed. Then he climbs in bed, lies on his back, and holds out his hand to me. When I take it, he helps me haul myself up onto the high bed and onto him.

I straddle him, positioning myself over his erection. He watches me with heated eyes as I grip his length and guide him into me. His flesh is hot and so hard in my grasp, it takes my breath away.

When I slowly sink down onto him, joining our bodies, he clamps his hands on my thighs and lets out a rough groan.

"Naked pregnant cowgirl," he says with a satisfied expression.

It's currently our favorite position. With my abdomen so big, there are only a couple of positions we can manage comfortably, and this is one of them.

Linking our fingers together, Shane steadies me as I start to move on him. I'm already so wet and aroused that it doesn't take me long to work him into me. I have the advantage in this position of being able to adjust the angle of penetration and the speed, so that he's hitting my g-spot perfectly. My body tightens on him, my sex squeezing his erection hard enough that he grits his teeth to keep from coming. As usual, he'll wait for me to come first. Then, and only then, will he give himself permission to seek his own pleasure.

My orgasm sweeps through me like a soft, rolling wave of heat and pleasure, and I cry out. He leans up to kiss me then, capturing the sounds I make and stealing my breath.

His big hands slide to my breasts, cupping them, and he teases my flushed nipples. He starts thrusting in earnest now, raising his hips and powering into me. My body is so soft and fluid, I'm half in a daze as the residual tremors of my climax sweep through me.

Shane has a lot of stamina, and normally he could go for ages, but I know he's worried about hurting me or wearing me out. So he lets himself come, his hips bucking into me with each spurt of his release. His hot flesh throbs deep inside me.

After his climax, he gently rolls me onto my side, and we lie facing each other. He threads his fingers in my hair as he kisses me, so gently and yet so thoroughly. My body melts into the bed, and for the moment, I'm relaxed and comforted.

When we hear a loud squawk over the baby monitor, followed by the rustling sound of the crib sheet, we both laugh.

Shane gets out of bed and heads to the bathroom to retrieve his clothes. "We just barely made it."

He stops long enough to pull on his jeans, commando. I give

him a little wave as he heads out of our bedroom on his way to our son's room, which is next to ours.

Pretty soon, our little family of three will become a family of four.

I smile as I stroke my belly.

* * *

A few minutes later, Shane returns with our son in his arms. I've slipped into a nightgown for decency and am sitting up in bed, leaning against the headboard.

"Mama," Luke cries as he reaches for me.

When Shane deposits him on the bed, Luke crawls to me and I intercept him before he can throw himself against me.

His little arms go around my neck, and he gives me a sloppy kiss on my cheek. "Mama."

"Hello, my sweet boy." I cuddle him close, breathing in his sweet baby smell and cherishing the moment. "Did you have a good nap?"

Luke pulls back to look me in the eye. "Eat."

I laugh "You're always hungry. Yes, we'll be eating soon."

Shane disappears into the closet and returns wearing a plain white T-shirt and carrying a pair of socks and sneakers. "Are you sure you're up for company tonight?" he asks me as he pulls on his socks. "We can cancel. I'm sure everyone will understand."

It's part of our normal routine—on Thursday evenings,

friends and family come over for dinner. We have an apartment full of people, lively entertainment, and good food. I wouldn't miss it for the world.

"Sure, I'm up for it. It'll probably be our last one for a while."

"If you're sure," he says again, sounding skeptical. "I don't want you overdoing it."

"I'm sure. I want to see everyone."

Shane takes Luke from me. "I'll go make his dinner while you get dressed."

As I watch them leave the room, I marvel at how well Shane has taken to fatherhood. He never hesitates to step up and do what needs to be done, whether it's feeding our son or changing a dirty diaper. I admit I'm spoiled. I have not only Shane to help me take care of Luke, but also our housemates, Sam and Cooper. They adore Luke and jump at any chance to take care of him.

After climbing out of bed, I make a quick visit to the bathroom, and then I change into a pair of stretchy maternity leggings and a big, loose top. When I join my family in the kitchen, Cooper is in the process of preparing a big batch of chicken wings to go into the air fryer.

"How ya feelin', kiddo?" he asks me when I walk into the room.

"Good. I had a nice soak in the tub while this little guy napped."

I nod to Luke, who is seated in his high chair at the kitchen counter. As I brush his pale blond hair, he reaches for my hand.

"Mama, eat," he says plaintively.

"Somebody sure is hungry," Cooper says with a wink to me. To Luke, he says, "It's comin', buddy. Hold your horses."

Sam joins us, carrying a number of empty beer cartons that have been flattened. He folds the cardboard carton and sticks it in the recycling bin. "The bar fridge is stocked," he says to Cooper. Then he sits on the stool next to Luke and ruffles his spikey blond hair. "Hey, little man. Did you have a good nap?"

Luke reaches up to do the same to Sam's red hair, but he can't quite reach that far, so Sam bends down to accommodate him. Luke laughs as he messes Sam's hair. Then he points across the kitchen, where Shane is preparing his dinner. "Eat!"

Sam laughs. "Be patient, little man. It's coming."

It's after five, and our guests will begin arriving any time. Usually, we're joined by Shane's siblings and their significant others, along with our friends and co-workers who live in the building—Mack and Erin, Philip, and Charlie. Mack's teenage daughter, Haley, also joins us on the weekends she spends with her dad and Erin.

"I think we'll have a full house tonight," Shane says as he checks his phone. "Everyone's confirming."

"I'd better put more wings on, then," Cooper says as he heads to the fridge. "These people sure do like to eat. I'll order some pizzas, too."

Shane brings Luke's plate to the counter and sets it down in front of him. On the toddler menu tonight is diced pieces of fruit, veggies, cheese, and thinly sliced turkey. Then he offers

Luke a sippy cup of milk.

Luke picks up his cup and drinks, then bangs it on the counter before setting it down and reaching for pieces of cut-up strawberries.

Shane stands behind me and wraps his arms around my thick waist. He leans down and whispers in my ear. "You look beautiful."

I smile. He makes me feel beautiful. But more importantly, he makes me feel loved.

2

Beth McIntyre

I love it when family comes to visit. Right now, our penthouse apartment is full to bursting. Everyone's in the rec room, eating, drinking, and laughing as they take bets on who will win the numerous skirmishes taking place in the boxing ring. My money is on two of Shane's brothers—Jamie and Liam—although Jake, Mack, and Dominic should never be underestimated because of their sheer size and strength. Still, my money is on Jamie, a former Navy SEAL, who in spite of his blindness, has uncanny skills when it comes to hand-to-hand combat. Also on Liam—the youngest McIntyre brother—a former international MMA champion.

I have a front row seat on one of the black leather sofas in the rec room. Currently, Shane is in the boxing ring with his brother Jake. It's a bit of an unfair skirmish as Jake is so much bigger than Shane. Jake outweighs Shane by at least thirty pounds of solid muscle. A corporate CEO versus a former heavy-weight boxer is pretty uneven. Still, Shane loves a challenge. And he especially loves sparring with his brothers.

I wince when Jake sneaks in a blow to Shane's left side. They're just boxing, with gloves and all, and headshots are off-limits. At least no one will get a concussion.

Jake's wife, Annie, is sitting beside me, and we're both devouring popcorn as we watch the match. Their three young children are back at home under the watchful eyes of Shane's parents.

When Jake manages to corner Shane and pummels him a bit, Annie hoots in support of her husband. "That's it, baby!" she yells, raising her fist in the air. "Show him who's boss." She grins at me. "He's such a *beast*."

I can tell from the tone of Annie's voice that she means that in a *very* good way. "TMI, Annie," I tease as I throw a piece of popcorn at her.

She throws a piece right back at me.

Erin's sitting on my other side. She grimaces whenever one of the guys manages to land a punch. Her boyfriend, Mack, is acting as the referee tonight, so he's in the ring with them. He's had to jump out of the way more than once to avoid getting caught in the crossfire.

Jake may be the bigger of the two, by far, but Shane does an admirable job of holding his own. After all, he spent ten years in the Marine Corps, in a special ops unit. Even though he's moved into corporate management, he's still got skills.

Cooper walks over from the bar and hands me a little plate of cheese slices and crackers and a glass of ice water. "You need to eat somethin', darlin'."

I smile as I accept the plate from the silver-haired man who's become like a father to me. "Yes, *Dad*."

"Don't sass me, young lady. You've got to keep your strength up. You haven't eaten much today. And you need to hydrate as well. Don't forget—you're eating and drinking for two."

Laughing, I lay a hand on my enormous baby bump as I gaze up into Cooper's smiling blue eyes. "I don't think I'm likely to forget that."

Cheers coming from the boxing ring draw our attention back to the match. Not surprisingly, Jake wins his skirmish with Shane. Liam steps into the ring next, to fight the winner. My money is definitely on Liam for this round. Jake's winded from going up against Shane, and Liam is a rarely defeated martial arts champion. While Jake has sheer brawn on his side, Liam is lean and fast.

As this new bout begins, I slip out of the noisy rec room and head to the kitchen on the pretense of resupplying the snack table. The real reason is my back is killing me, and I need a quiet moment alone to regroup.

I fill my glass with some ice-cold, fresh-squeezed orange juice and take a seat on one of the breakfast bar stools. Just as I sit, a sharp twinge in my abdomen nearly doubles me over.

"Calm down, peanut," I say, my breath trapped in my chest. I press a hand to my rock-hard belly and feel the baby squirming. A moment later, the baby kicks me in the ribs, practically knocking the air out of me.

While I'm trying to catch my breath, I hear someone calling my name. It's Molly, Jamie's girlfriend.

"In the kitchen," I tell her. I paste a smile onto my face.

Molly comes around the corner, into the kitchen, followed by Shane's eldest sister, Sophie, who's about four months pregnant and just starting to show.

Molly stands across the counter from me, gathering her long, wavy brown hair off her neck as she observes me. "Do you need any help?"

"Thanks, but no. I'm just taking a break."

When the baby kicks my ribs again, I grab hold of the edge of the counter. Then, as the twinge of pain returns and I feel my abdomen tighten, I blow out a long breath and silently count to three. *Don't panic. You're okay.*

Molly lays her hand on mine. "Are you okay?"

Wincing, I nod. "It's just the usual baby shenanigans."

Lia walks into the kitchen then—Shane's youngest sister—her pretty face flushed and sweaty. She's wearing her typical workout gear—black boy shorts and a matching sports bra—and her blonde hair is braided to stay out of her face. She's spent her fair share of time in the boxing ring this evening with her brothers, giving them a good run for their money. Lia may be petite, but she's fierce. "Need more beer," she says.

I point to the oversized, industrial refrigerator. "In there."

Lia grabs a carton, sets it on the counter, and pauses to study me. "You look like shit, princess. What's wrong?"

I force a smile I don't quite feel as the pressure on my abdomen increases. "I'm just resting."

I wince as a band tightens steadily around my abdomen, making it hard to breathe. I can't help remembering back to when my water broke when I was pregnant with Luke. Lia and I were hiding in the attic of a convenience store that was currently being robbed by armed men. Lia saved me and my baby.

Lia's blue eyes narrow sharply. "Something's wrong."

The moment she says that, a wave of pressure envelops me, and I have to bite my lip to keep from gasping.

Molly and Sophie, who've both been observing quietly, step closer.

"Beth? Are you sure you're all right?" Sophie asks.

As the pressure increases, I find myself panting through it. *In, out. In, out.*

Lia scowls at me. "Fuck. You're in labor. Why the hell didn't you say something?"

"It just now started. I'm not even sure it's actually labor. It could be Braxton-Hicks contractions. God knows I get those often enough."

Jonah Locke comes around the corner, his gaze going right

to Lia, his fiancée. "Hey, tiger. Did you find the beer?"

Lia points at the carton sitting on the counter. "Yeah, but we have more important issues to deal with."

When Jonah gets a good look at me, his smile falters. "Is everything okay?"

Lia elbows him. "No, everything's not okay. Princess is in labor."

"Seriously?" Jonah's dark eyes widen. "Shit. Does Shane know?"

"No one knows," Lia says. "It just started."

Cooper comes around the corner carrying two empty food trays. "We need more cheese and crackers—" He stops dead in his tracks and stares at me. "Damn it, kiddo, why didn't you say something?" He hands the empty trays to Molly, turns on his heel, and walks back the way he came.

Lia grins. "Wait for it. Three, two—"

Shane comes storming into the kitchen, his face flushed from physical exertion. His short brown hair is damp with sweat and matted to his head, and he has the beginnings of a black eye, a bloody lip, and a one-inch cut on his cheekbone. His gaze sweeps me from head to toe. "Sweetheart."

I smile weakly. "Hi, honey."

Instantly, his demeanor transforms from family man to CEO, and he barks out orders. "Sam, get the Escalade. Sophie, call Mom and Dad and Ingrid. Cooper, call Tyler."

Sam appears, my best friend and bodyguard, his posture on full alert. He takes one look at me and heads for the elevator that will take him down to the parking garage where our vehicles are kept.

Shane steps directly in front of me and gazes into my eyes. "Are you in pain?"

"A little." But I can't say much more because there's still a vise squeezing my belly tight. All I can do is focus on breathing.

"You're having contractions?" he asks.

"I think so." When I feel a rush of warm water between my legs, I glance down. "My water just broke."

"Okay, we're going," Shane says calmly. Carefully, he lifts me into his arms. "Sorry, guys," he calls out to everyone within hearing distance. "Party's over. We're having a baby. Let yourselves out."

Cooper appears, holding Shane's wallet, phone, and a change of clothes. "Go," he says. "Everyone knows their jobs. I've got Luke."

My heart wrenches at the thought of leaving my baby boy behind—since he came home from the hospital, we've never been apart. My only comfort is in knowing Luke idolizes Cooper. He'll be perfectly fine at home with his *Hooper*.

As Shane carries me to the elevator, we're accompanied by Lia, who's carrying my overnight bag, which has been packed and ready to go for the past two weeks.

"I'm having a serious case of déjà vu," she says with a frown.

I know she's thinking back to when Luke was born under horrible conditions.

Then she snaps out of it. "It won't be like the last time," she assures me. "Don't worry about a thing. Just go have a baby."

I manage a smile, but the truth is I'm scared.

"This time it'll be textbook perfect," she says as if she's reading my mind. "Trust me."

Shane carries me into the elevator, and I wave at the concerned crowd seeing us off as the elevator doors close.

"I'm scared," I confess. I can't seem to stop shaking.

I keep thinking about when Luke was born. I'd never been so scared in my life. If Jason Miller hadn't been able to get Luke breathing, we might have lost him. Our poor baby boy was in the neonatal intensive care for so long, and I struggled so badly to nurse him or even bond with him. I'm just praying I won't experience post-partum depression again like I did the first time.

Shane tightens his hold on me and kisses my temple. "It's going to be fine, I promise. I won't leave your side. Not for a minute."

I still can't stop shaking though.

3

Beth McIntyre

Shane punches the elevator button, and the doors close. As we begin to descend, he says, "Do you think you can stand for a few minutes?"

"Yes." The crushing weight on my abdomen has eased.

He sets me on my feet and then quickly changes into the clean clothes that Cooper handed him on our way out. He wipes his face and neck on his workout T-shirt. "That'll have to do until I get a chance to shower." He studies me. "How are you feeling?"

"Better. The contraction's over."

He pulls me into his arms, and I feel his lips against my ear. "Just relax. Everything's going to be fine. We'll be holding our new baby girl before you know it."

I laugh, just as he had intended. "Or boy."

His chest vibrates as he chuckles. "Whatever you say, sweetheart. I know better than to argue with a pregnant woman."

When the elevator doors open, Shane picks up my overnight bag and takes my hand. Parked right outside the elevator is the Escalade. As we approach, Sam jumps out of the driver's side and comes around to open the rear passenger door. Shane sets my overnight bag on the floor and lifts me into his arms to set me on the seat.

"I'll get it wet," I warn him, reminding him of my broken water and soaked clothing.

"It's fine, honey," he says as he lowers me onto the seat and reaches for my seat belt. After he fastens me in, he jogs around to the other side of the vehicle and climbs in beside me.

We're off a moment later as Sam drives us to the hospital.

I lean my head back in my seat and close my eyes as I try to focus on remaining calm. The last thing I need right now is to have a panic attack.

As I blow out a long, shaky breath, Shane reaches for my hand and links our fingers together. "Just keep breathing, sweetheart. I'll be with you every second. Everything's going to be fine."

I'm not sure which one of us he's trying to convince—himself or me.

His voice is low and steady, but I'm sure he's thinking back to the last time.

* * *

It is different this time. I'm surrounded by hospital staff—a labor and delivery nurse, Emma; and my regular obstetrician, Dr. Shaw, who is on hospital duty this evening. My husband is at my side, and my mom is in the delivery room with us. My brother and his boyfriend are out in the waiting room, along with Shane's entire family. Shane's middle sister, Hannah, is booking the first flight she can catch from Denver to Chicago.

"You're doing great," Emma says. My labor and delivery nurse is a middle-aged woman with brown hair pulled up in a bun and kind brown eyes framed by tiny laugh lines. She studies the row of machines next to me—the ones keeping track of my pulse and blood pressure and the contractions. "Get ready, Beth," she warns. "Another one's coming."

Shane's fingers tighten on mine. He's been at my side every second, often in my line of sight as he talks me through the contractions. He's strong, and yet compassionate, and when I begin to falter, he shows me tough love. Still, I feel the occasional tremor in his hand and the anxiety lurking behind his beautiful blue eyes. He's scared, too; he just won't admit it. We're both still fixating on how close we came to losing Luke.

A wave of crushing pressure sweeps over my abdomen, and my ability to breathe goes right out the window.

"It's okay, baby," Mom says as she takes my other hand in hers. She's standing on the other side of my bed, opposite Shane. "You can do this, darling. Just breathe through it."

But it's hard to breathe when you can't get any air into your lungs. I can't tell if it's the contraction I'm feeling or if I'm having an asthma attack. The pressure is so tight, as if there's a steel band wrapped around my torso, tightening, constricting my air. Thank goodness for the epidural—the pain's not so bad. It's the pressure.

"Breathe, sweetheart," Shane says in a calm, low voice. "You have to breathe."

I realize I'm holding my breath. "I can't," I rasp out.

He bites back a smile. "Yes, you can, honey. Just try to relax and breathe through the contraction."

"I'd like to see you try this!" I say, perhaps considerably louder than I meant to. I know he's just trying to be helpful, but right now, I don't think anything can help me.

He tries hard not to laugh, but I can see the amusement in his eyes. I don't think I've ever yelled at him before.

"Stop smiling, Shane! It's not funny."

His lips flatten into a line. "I'm not smiling, I promise."

As the peak of the contraction hits me, I lean back onto the pillow, close my eyes, and grit my teeth. I don't remember it being this hard.

Mom brushes her soft fingertips across my hot, clammy forehead. "You're doing beautifully, darling," she says in her soft voice. The soft lilt of her Swedish accent comforts me.

I'm so glad she's here with me this time. Through no fault of her own, she missed Luke's birth. My throat tightens. "Mom."

"It's okay, baby," she says as she strokes my hair back from my face.

Shane cups my left hand in both of his, and his lips press against my knuckles. As he gazes at me with eyes that burn with emotion, I realize this is just as hard on him as it is on me.

As the contraction begins to ease, the nurse pats my leg. "Try to rest now, Beth, before the next contraction. It won't be long now. I'll go get Dr. Shaw."

I exhale a long breath and relax into the mattress. I can breathe easier now.

"You're doing so well, baby," Mom says, smiling as she leans forward to kiss the side of my head. "It won't be much longer now. You'll be holding your sweet little baby in your arms before you know it."

Smiling, I nod. "I don't remember it being this hard."

Mom laughs. "Honey, nature has a way of softening a woman's memory when it comes to childbirth. If it didn't, humans would have died out a long time ago."

I laugh. "You must be right. Look at how many babies Bridget has had. Annie, too."

I turn to face my husband, who's uncharacteristically silent. "How are you holding up?"

He laughs. "Shouldn't I be the one asking you that?"

I squeeze his hand. "I know this is hard on you, too."

As he kisses my hand, his eyes radiate tension. "You have no idea, sweetheart."

4

Shane McIntyre

A sense of calm has stolen over me, much to my surprise—and relief. I realize Beth needs me to be calm because she's scared to death.

The moment I realized she was in labor, my heart practically stopped. Even now, I have to keep reminding myself this isn't like the last time. This baby is full term—ready to be born—and Beth is in a great state of mind. She's giving birth in a hospital, under the supervision of her obstetrician.

This time will be different. It has to be. I can't bear for her to go through again what she experienced the last time.

Beth's been in labor for a number of hours now... I've lost count. I glance at a clock on the wall to see that it's three in the morning. She's been at this for nearly six hours.

Dr. Shaw returns to check on Beth's progress. She's been in and out of our room all night. Finally, this time, after a quick examination, she informs us that Beth is dilated to nine centimeters—it's time.

Beth's poor mother, Ingrid, looks paler than usual. She's been at Beth's side since she arrived, holding her daughter's hand, giving her words of encouragement. Ingrid has claimed her spot on the right side of Beth's bed, and I'm on her left. We're both holding one of Beth's hands. When the contractions come, hard and fast, Beth squeezes my hand so tightly she cuts off my circulation.

"You need to breathe, Beth," Emma says as she monitors Beth's vitals. "Take some deep breaths. You need oxygen, as does your baby. Try not to hold your breath."

Emma's a god-send. Being a mother herself—she's told us about her own kids—she knows exactly what Beth is going through. And she has a calming, reassuring demeanor that we all need right now.

Emma glances at one of the machines that monitor Beth's contractions. "Get ready, sweetie. Here comes another one."

As Beth grimaces through the wave, Dr. Shaw checks on the baby.

"I can feel the baby's head," Shaw says. "It's about to crown. Beth, can you bear down now and give me a big push?"

Beth's lips are compressed in a line as she strains so hard her face turns bright red.

My heart thuds painfully in my chest. God, I wish I could do this for her. If I could take the pain from her, I would. Gladly.

All night, Beth's contractions have ebbed and flowed like ocean waves sweeping onto shore, then retreating. Even with the epidural, she's still feeling quite a bit of discomfort. Time seems to have stilled. My sole focus right now is on my wife, and I do whatever I can to comfort and reassure her, just as her mother does.

Periodically, Ingrid and I make eye contact across the bed. I see the concern in her eyes—the worry for her daughter—and I know we're feeling the same emotions. I give her a reassuring nod, and she replies with a grateful smile.

Dr. Shaw starts getting excited, her voice rising in pitch as she fires out instructions. "One more time, Beth. You can do it—you're so close. Give me one more really good push."

I move in closer and support Beth as she leans forward into a determined push. She strains so hard I'm afraid she's going to pop a blood vessel.

"That's it, sweetheart," I tell her, leaning in to support her from behind. "You're doing great."

With a fierce growl, Beth gives all she's got. The only thing I can do to help her is murmur encouragement and hold her tight.

A moment later, Dr. Shaw holds up a small infant in her hands, the baby's skin mottled red and wrinkled. She holds the baby in her palm, face down, and rubs the infant's back. I think we're all holding our breath as we wait for a sign that the baby is breathing.

Please, just a tiny sound.
A breath.
A cry.
A loud squawk.
Anything.

My heart is pounding, and I can't help thinking back to when Luke was born. He didn't cry. He didn't make a sound, and I'd been so afraid for him. Afraid for my wife. It took some doing for Jason Miller to finally get Luke breathing.

I spare a moment to look at Beth. She's frozen, staring at the baby, her eyes wide, and I know exactly what's going through her mind.

Not again.

I hug her. "It's all right, sweetheart. It's going to be fine."

Seeming perfectly unconcerned, Dr. Shaw continues to rub our baby's back. Calmly, patiently, she pats the baby, then gives it a tiny nudge. Shaw turns the baby over and suctions fluid from the its mouth. Suddenly, we hear a gasp, then a sputter, followed by a wet cough. And then comes the best sound of all—a thin, reedy cry as our baby takes its first breath.

"Who do we have here?" Dr. Shaw muses as she turns the baby over and skims her gaze over the tiny little body. "Ah, a little girl. And she looks absolutely perfect. Ten little fingers and ten little toes. Congratulations, you two."

A girl.

We have a daughter.

I open my mouth to tease Beth that I was right, but she slumps weakly in my arms, and I gently lay her back on the mattress.

With a sigh, Beth closes her eyes.

I brush her hair back from her frighteningly pale face. "Sweetheart? Are you okay?" When she doesn't respond, my tone sharpens. "Beth, look at me."

Her blue-green eyes flutter open, and she gives me a weak smile. "You were right."

Relief floods me as I return her smile. "We have a daughter."

"Shane?" Dr. Shaw offers me a pair of surgical scissors. "Would you like to do the honors?"

Immediately, my mind flashes back to Luke's birth when I cut his umbilical cord, but under very different circumstances. But this is a different time, a different place, and a different delivery. Right now, our daughter is red-faced and squalling with indignation. It's the most beautiful sound I've heard in a long time.

I gaze down at the umbilical cord, which is already clamped in two places.

"Cut here," she says, pointing to a spot between the clamps.

My hand shakes as I cut the cord. Then Shaw lays the baby on Beth's bare chest and covers them with a blanket.

Beth's arms come up to cradle the baby, who's already nuzzling at her breast. "Hello there, little darling," she says as she strokes the baby's hair, which is a fine dusting of brown peach fuzz. Beth gives me a radiant smile. "Brown hair, just like yours."

The sight of my wife holding our newborn daughter makes me choke up.

My girls.

As the baby wriggles and fusses, Beth speaks softly as she tries to comfort her. A moment later, the baby is rooting around, clearly looking for a nipple to latch onto. Beth guides the tip of her breast to the baby's mouth, and after a few awkward tries, the baby manages to latch on.

I watch, mesmerized, as the baby attempts to suckle. I know Beth's milk won't come for a while, but at least the baby gets colostrum.

Beth rubs the baby's back as she nurses, speaking softly. I think back to how Beth struggled to nurse Luke, how frustrated she became. This time, it seems almost effortless.

Beth grins up at me. "Isn't she perfect?"

I nod, too choked up to speak.

Soon after, Dr. Shaw asks to borrow our baby for just a few minutes. She lays her in a clear acrylic bassinet, and after wiping her clean performs a quick exam, checking her vitals.

"Six pounds two ounces," Shaw says, as she returns the baby to Beth's arms. "Twenty inches long. She looks fantastic, guys."

Ingrid's eyes tear up as she watches Beth holding our new baby. "I'm so happy for you both."

A little while later, Emma tells us she's going to take our baby away for a bath and a more thorough examination. "I'll bring her back as soon as that's done."

Beth grabs my arm. "Go with her, Shane. Don't let her out of your sight. Promise me."

"I promise," I say as I kiss my wife's forehead before following our daughter into the hallway.

* * *

I escort Emma to the delivery nursery where she gives our baby her first bath. I have an identification bracelet on my wrist, as does Beth. The baby now has a tiny little tag around her ankle identifying her as Baby Girl McIntyre.

As Emma gently washes her, I finally get a good chance to study our tiny, wriggling baby. Her face is round, her nose a perfect little button. She vigorously kicks her legs and arms as she blinks up at the overhead lights.

I reach out with my index finger to touch one of her hands. When she grasps my finger, my heart thuds hard in my chest. I'm swamped with an overwhelming sense of responsibility and love for this precious little being.

"Is she your first?" Emma asks.

"No. We have a son, fifteen months old."

She smiles. "One of each, then. How nice. Do you have a name picked out for your daughter?"

"I think we do. My wife and I mulled over some ideas. Now that she's born, and we know she's a girl, we'll have to finalize our choice and make it official."

When the bath is over, Emma diapers the baby and dresses her in a white cotton onesie before wrapping her in a soft blanket. "Shall we take this little girl back to her mama?"

We arrive back at the room with the baby in her bassinet, just as another nurse is helping Beth get cleaned up. Ingrid rests in her chair beside the bed, holding Beth's hand.

As soon as she spots me, Beth holds out her free hand. I take it in both of mine and lean down to kiss it.

"How is she?" she asks in a hoarse voice. She sounds exhausted.

"She's perfect."

I lean over her, smiling and brushing her hair back from her hot, damp face. "I'm so proud of you."

She gives me a teary smile. "I couldn't have done it without you."

* * *

An hour later, just before dawn, Beth is asleep, as is the baby. I've taken a quick shower and dressed into clothes Cooper dropped off for me. I turn the lights down low and close the blinds to darken the room so Beth can sleep. She needs rest now more than anything.

Ingrid goes downstairs to the cafeteria with her son, Tyler, and Tyler's fiancé, Ian, to grab something to eat and a cup of coffee. Tyler and Ian have been here all night in the waiting room.

The baby's rolling bassinet stands at the foot of Beth's bed. I'm seated on a chair beside the bed, my attention split between my wife and our daughter.

I check the time. I imagine Luke will be awake before long, if he's not already. He's an early riser like me. As our family grows, so do my responsibilities. Beth and I now have two children to worry about. I don't know how my parents managed with seven.

Cooper steps into the room and comes to stand beside the bassinet. He stares long and hard at the baby, then at Beth. "How's she doing?" he asks quietly so as not to wake her. He nods toward Beth.

I nod. "Pretty well. She's exhausted."

He comes to stand by my chair and clamps his hand on my shoulder, giving it a squeeze. "Congratulations, buddy. Sam's sending me regular updates on Luke—he's doing fine. I'll go back out to the waiting room and let you get some rest."

I follow Cooper's advice and take a quick catnap in a reclining chair while I can. I know it's only a matter of time before visitors start showing up in droves, wanting to see the new baby and congratulate us.

A couple hours later, there's a light tap on the door, and then my parents walk into the room, their expressions eager.

"Can we come in?" my mom asks as she peers into the dimly-lit room.

"Of course," I say in a quiet voice, holding a finger to my lips. "Beth's sleeping."

Mom nods. "We'll be quiet. I just need to see my new granddaughter."

Mom peeks at Beth, who's sleeping. Then she and Dad both move to the bassinet and gaze down at the sleeping baby.

Mom grins at me. "Congratulations, honey," she whispers. "Can I hold her?"

"Of course."

Mom picks the baby up and cradles her gently. "Have you guys picked out a name?"

"We agreed on a girl's name, but I need to discuss it with Beth before we announce it. I want to make sure she hasn't changed her mind."

My parents take a seat on the sofa to cuddle with the baby. When Beth stirs, I return to my chair beside her bed.

"Hi," I say quietly when she opens her eyes.

She smiles tiredly. "How is she?"

"She's fine. She's still sleeping." I nod across the room to my folks. "My parents are here." I reach for Beth's hand, which is soft and cool in mine. "We should finalize her name."

Beth smiles. "I like Ava. Ava McIntyre."

"Ava *Elizabeth* McIntyre," I say. "After her mom." I lean forward and kiss Beth, my lips gentle on hers. She's been through so much, I just want to wrap her up in my arms and keep her safe. "Did you guys hear that?" I call to my parents. "Her name is Ava Elizabeth."

My mom beams. "Little Ava. That's perfect. I love it."

Throughout the day, there's a quiet parade of people in and out of Beth's room. Tyler and Ian come to the room to see Beth and the baby. My siblings all come to visit, except for Hannah, who hasn't arrived yet from Colorado. Sam and Cooper come to visit. Molly and Jamie are at the penthouse watching Luke.

Everyone can tell that Beth is exhausted, so they keep their visits short and sweet. Once Beth and Ava are released from the hospital, I'm taking them and Luke straight to our home in Kenilworth. That's where Beth will recuperate. Our family and friends will join us there to help us celebrate.

That evening, Tyler and Ian take Ingrid home so she can get some much-needed rest. Finally, it's just the two of us—well, the three of us.

The nurse helps Beth get up and walk to the restroom. Post-delivery, Beth's definitely doing better than she did when Luke was born, which is a huge relief. I didn't want her to have to go through so much trauma as she did last time.

Beth wakes up twice in the night to the cries of a fussy baby and attempts to nurse Ava. It's hit or miss. Beth is experienced after having nursed Luke for a year, but it's always touchy with a new baby who hasn't quite learned how to properly latch on. The baby gets frustrated and cries a lot, which distresses Beth.

I try to be helpful, but there's not much I can do except be supportive. After another attempted nursing, I change Ava's diaper and dress her in a clean onesie—this one a soft pink with white bunnies on it. It's a gift from Tyler and Ian, meaning Ian must have picked it out. I can't see Tyler shopping for baby clothes.

After dressing Ava, I wrap her in a soft, white baby blanket.

Ava is wide awake now, so I hold her for a while, just talking to her. I tell her about her big brother, who's going to love her. I tell her about her cousins—Aiden, Everly, and Emerly—who she will meet soon. I tell her about her godfathers, Cooper and Sam, who she met briefly today, and all about her many uncles and aunts.

After Ava falls asleep in my arms, I tuck her into the bassinet. Then, utterly exhausted, I drop down into the chair beside Beth's bed.

"Happy?" Beth says quietly as she glances my way.

I turn to see her smiling at me. "Very."

There are tears in her eyes when she says, "Me too."

She pats the mattress. "Lie down with me."

"I'm afraid there's not enough room. I don't want to crush you."

She smiles as she reaches for my hand. "There's always enough room for spooning."

I kick off my shoes and climb onto the bed to lie behind her and spoon her.

She sighs contentedly as I hold her close. "This is so much better."

While I hold her in my arms, Beth drifts off to sleep. I'm exhausted, too, but sleep doesn't come easily. My mind is reeling. We have *two* children now. Two babies. The thought hits me like a ton of bricks.

Two.

I want to be a good dad, not just now while they're babies, but later, too, when they're grown.

I want a relationship with them like I have with my parents. My dad has always been a good role model. Now it's my turn.

5

Beth McIntyre

I wake after a long nap, groggy and a bit disoriented. Shane is sitting in the chair beside my bed, holding Ava to his chest. He's gazing down at her sweet little face, speaking softly to her. It's hard to believe Luke was once that small—smaller, in fact, as he was born prematurely.

Quietly, I observe father and daughter. I'm glad to see that she has his brown hair. "She's perfect, isn't she?"

He glances up at the sound of my voice.

It's then I see the glitter of tears in his eyes. "What's wrong?"

Tears spill over onto his cheeks. "You've given me everything,

Beth. Everything I could possibly want." He rises up from his chair, Ava cradled carefully in his arms, and leans close to kiss me. "I'm a very lucky man."

My throat tightens painfully. "I think you got it backward. I'm the lucky one." He's made it possible for me to love and be loved. That's something I thought I could never have.

* * *

Saturday morning, Lia stops by for a visit. She drops down into the chair beside my bed and peers across the room to the sofa, where both our moms are fawning over Ava. "You've got another cute baby, princess."

Hearing Lia call me *princess* makes me smile. The nickname she gave me when we first met has stuck.

"So, how are you feeling after pushing her out?" she asks me.

She makes a face as she shudders, probably thinking back to the day Luke was born. Lia was there with me every step of the way.

I laugh. "Much better than last time."

There's a flash of pain in Lia's blue eyes, and it reminds me of the dire circumstances we found ourselves in the day Luke was born. Lia saved my life that day, and ultimately Luke's life, too. I owe her everything.

Shane's youngest sister props her boots on the metal bed frame as she sips a Starbucks coffee. "Jonah sends his love. He really wanted to come see you and the baby, but he was afraid his presence here at the hospital would cause too much of a ruckus. He says he's sorry and that he'll see you and Ava soon at the big house."

"Please tell him it's okay. I totally understand."

Jonah Locke draws huge crowds wherever he goes—screaming teenagers by the hundreds. I guess that's one of the downsides to being a rockstar. It only takes one fan to notice him out in public before the news is plastered all over social media, and the fans show up in droves. He's easy to spot… hot guy with a manbun and tats. It's not easy for him to fly under the radar screen.

When Ava makes a squeak, we both turn to look at her across the room. The two grandmothers are seated on the sofa, along with Luke. My mom's now holding her very first granddaughter while Shane's mom, Bridget, holds Luke.

Luke is uncharacteristically subdued as he stares in wonder at his baby sister.

"Is this your baby sister?" my mom asks him. "Is this baby Ava?"

Luke points at Ava. "Baby."

"Yes, she's your baby sister, Ava. Can you say *Ava*?"

Luke points again. "Baby."

Cooper stopped by first thing this morning to bring us Luke. When Cooper carried him into my room and he spotted me and Shane, Luke burst into tears. He cuddled with me on my bed for a good long while.

Since he's her sibling, Luke's allowed to be here in the room with us. Right now, Shane's out in the visiting room chatting with the rest of our family and friends who stopped by. I'm sure he's showing them some of the dozens of pictures he's taken of her.

Later that morning, Dr. Shaw stops by to examine me and gives me a gold star. The pediatrician who's on call stops in to see Ava. She gets a gold star, too. Now we're just waiting for the both of us to be released so we can head to our home in Kenilworth, north of the city. I can't wait to get there so we can relax for a couple of days with our family and friends.

* * *

Late afternoon, I get the go-ahead to leave the hospital. Sam and Cooper have already packed our bags for us, and everything we and the kids will need has already been delivered to the house in Kenilworth. Shane will drive me and the kids, while Sam and Cooper follow us in another vehicle.

Once we're on the road, I keep looking to the back seat to check on both kids. Luke is playing with his favorite stuffed kitty cat. Ava dozed off as soon as we reached the highway.

As Shane watches me watching the kids, he reaches for my hand and brings it to his mouth to kiss. "I love you," he says with so much emotion and sincerity my heart aches.

I squeeze his hand. "I love you, too."

He tips his head toward the back seat. "We made those two kids."

"I know. I was there, remember?"

He laughs. "I remember every second of it." He lays my hand on his thigh and covers it with his own. "I don't know what I'd do without you." He shoots me a quick glance. "You've given me a life and a family I only dreamed of."

Shane's a decade older than I am, and he had ample opportunity to get married before we met. In fact, I've met a couple of the women who would have gladly said yes to him if he'd asked them.

My eyes tear up as I turn my palm over and link my fingers with his. He's given *me* everything—he gave me back my life at a time when anxiety and fear ruled it. Because of him, I've had a chance to grow and spread my wings without fear.

* * *

When we arrive at our home in Kenilworth, on a lovely September evening, it's still light outside. Elly and George Peterson, the caretakers of this estate, come out the front door before Shane shuts off the engine.

Elly opens my door and helps me out of the vehicle. Then she pulls me gently into her arms for a hug. "Oh, sweetie, congratulations." She releases me so she can peek through the rear passenger window at the kids, both of whom are sleeping.

Elly waves to her husband. "George, come look at her. She's absolutely precious. And look how big Luke has gotten. It seems like it's been ages since we've seen him."

"The new nursery is ready," George says proudly. "And the baby's bassinet is assembled and ready for use."

Shane asked George a while back to have someone cut a door through our bedroom wall to connect our room with the one next to ours. Now we have a two-room suite that includes an attached nursery for Luke. Ava will sleep in the bassinet beside our bed until she's a little older.

Shane claps George on the shoulder. "Thank you. I can't wait to see how it turned out."

"It was all my pleasure," George says.

Sam and Cooper, who pulled in right behind us, exit their vehicle and join us.

Cooper peers into the back seat. "They're both asleep?" He chuckles. "We'll see how long that lasts."

As soon as he opens the rear passenger door, Luke's eyes pop open. "Hoop!"

While Cooper unbuckles Luke from his car seat, Shane opens the other passenger door and retrieves Ava's car seat. She's still sound asleep.

"Come inside, everyone," Elly says as she heads for the door and holds it open for us. "Are you hungry? I can fix you something real quick if you don't want to wait for dinner to be served."

"Thank you, but I'll wait," I say. Right now, I need to lie

down. "We'll take the kids up to our room first and get them settled in."

As he follows me inside the house, Shane leans over and kisses Elly's soft, wrinkled cheek. "Would you send up a tray for Beth?" he says in a low voice. "She hasn't eaten much today."

Elly nods. "I will."

Not wanting to deal with the stairs right now, I head for the elevator. Shane, who's carrying Ava, joins me. Sam and Cooper head up the stairs with Luke. The elevator is slow as molasses, so it's not surprising that the guys beat us up to our suite. I'm eager to see what the nursery renovation looks like.

When we enter our room, we can hear Sam and Cooper talking in the adjoining nursery. Shane sets Ava's car seat on our bed, and we follow the sounds of voices.

Luke is standing in the crib, holding onto the railing as he bounces on the mattress, squealing with glee.

I do a quick survey of the room—two cribs, a padded rocking chair for nursing, a bookcase filled with children's books, a basket of toys, a shelf of stuffed animals, and new plush carpeting underfoot. The nursery has its own private bathroom.

Like our room, the nursery overlooks the rear lawn that sweeps down to Lake Michigan and our private beach and dock.

"This is perfect," I say, taking it all in.

Sam and Cooper leave us to settle into our room. Luke is wide awake now after his impromptu nap on the drive here. Ava is still sleeping, so I remove her from her car seat and lay her in the bassinet positioned right next to my side of the bed.

My milk has started coming in, so I hope she'll wake up soon and nurse.

"Lie down and rest, sweetheart," Shane says. "I'll keep Luke entertained."

I doze off for about forty-five minutes before Ava wakes up and starts crying. When I sit up, I notice there's a cart sitting at the foot of our bed. On it is a plate of cheese and crackers, along with a bowl of fresh berries, courtesy of Elly, I'm sure. I pop a strawberry into my mouth before I pick up Ava and take her into the nursery for a diaper change.

Shane is seated on the carpet in the nursery, putting a little wooden train set together for Luke. Luke is beside himself with excitement, too eager to wait for Shane to finish. As soon as Shane connects two pieces of the train track, Luke reaches for them and pulls them apart.

Shane laughs. "He's not quite figured out how trains work."

After I change Ava's diaper, I sit with her on the rocking chair and nurse her while Shane and Luke play.

I don't think life can get much better than this.

6

Liam McIntyre

It looks like I'm the first to arrive, besides the guests of honor. I spot Shane's Escalade parked in the spacious circular drive in front of the house, along with the Mercedes. I imagine Sam and Cooper are here too. But I don't see any others yet. I know my folks are on their way—and they're bringing Beth's mom. They'll be here any minute.

The sun is just starting to set, and the horizon is turning shades of orange and pink. I grab my overnight bag from my truck and jog up the front steps. I'm looking forward to hanging with my entire family under one roof for a couple of days. Even

Hannah will be here.

George Peterson is just coming out of the house as I open the front door. As usual, he's dressed in dusty overalls, a plaid shirt, and well-worn work boots. His silver hair is buzzed military short.

"Hello, young man," he says in his gruff voice as he clamps a hand on my shoulder. "Shane and Beth are up in their room with their kids. That baby girl sure is a cutie."

Just as I walk inside, I spot Elly scurrying through the wide-open foyer as she heads toward the kitchen. When I get a whiff of what's cooking, my stomach growls in anticipation.

"Hello, Liam!" she calls, sounding a bit winded. "Sorry, dear, but I need to get the rolls out of the oven. Dinner's at seven-thirty."

I wave in her direction. "No problem." And then I climb the stairs to the second floor and head down the hallway to my room, where I dump my duffle bag beside the bed.

First things first... I need to pay my respects to the newest member of the family. Just as Shane predicted, they had a girl. I'm sure he's happy, but it looks like I'm out a hundred bucks. Some of the guys at work bet on whether or not Shane was right about the baby's gender. I should have known better than to bet against my big bro.

After dumping my gear off in my room, I head down the hall to theirs. Their door is open, and I hear voices inside—Sam's and Cooper's.

I knock. "Can I come in?"

"Liam! Come on in," Shane calls from the adjoining room.

I'd heard he was having the room next to theirs connected so they could use it for a nursery.

I can't believe how quickly our family has grown in the past couple of years, going from zero grandkids to now five of them, what with Jake's three kids and now Shane's two. And my sister Sophie is due sometime early next year, and that will bring the count to six. That's crazy. Although I guess it's to be expected from a family with seven kids. Our parents sure are happy about all these grandkids.

I pass through the bedroom and into the nursery, where I find Shane, Sam, and Cooper seated on the floor with Luke, playing with a little wooden train set. That looks like my old Thomas the Train, if I'm not mistaken. When I was young, I was determined to grow up to be a train conductor. Didn't happen. Instead, I followed a more grown-up dream to go into mixed martial arts, which is what I love. There's nothing I'd rather do than compete and teach martial arts. I empower people to strive for their physical best. To protect themselves.

Beth is seated in a rocking chair, and presumably their new baby is in her arms. I can't exactly tell as she has a thin blanket slung over her chest and shoulder, probably because she's nursing the baby.

Shane waves me over. "Perfect timing, Liam. You're the family train expert. Come join us."

"No, it goes like this," Cooper says as he rearranges two pieces. "See? Now it fits."

As soon as he spots me, my nephew Luke shoots to his feet and runs over to me before wrapping his arms around my shins. He grabs my hand and pulls me toward the train set, motioning for me to sit down and join them.

"Is this my old train set?" I ask, pretty sure it is. I scan the toy cars and the wooden accessories, the track pieces, a little bridge, wooden pine trees, and railroad crossing signs.

Shane nods as he connects two pieces of track. "Mom found it in the attic and gave it to us." He gives me a look. "Unless you want it back?"

I shake my head and laugh. "No, Luke can have it. Nice shiner, by the way." Shane is sporting a bit of a black eye.

He gives me an annoyed look. "Gee, thanks. If I'm not mistaken, I have you to thank for it."

He's not wrong. He ducked just as I executed a roundhouse kick when we were hanging out at the penthouse Thursday evening. My foot caught the edge of his cheek, just beneath his eye. He's lucky I didn't crack the socket. Once I realized what was happening, I pulled my punch; otherwise, it would have been much worse. I guess he's slowing down a bit in his old age, now that he's married and the father of two.

Speaking of two kids… I glance behind me at Beth, who's still nursing. I guess I'll have to wait a bit before I can greet my new niece.

"So, three girls now and two boys," I say.

"Maybe Sophie will have a boy and even up the count," Beth says.

My oldest sister, Sophie, who recently married Dominic Zaretti, is around four months pregnant. The pregnancy occurred well *before* they eloped, but I'm not judging. My sister seems really happy, and that's all that matters. And it's obvious how Dominic feels. He dotes on her.

Beth lowers the baby blanket and buttons up her top. Then she props the baby against her shoulder and pats her back. We hear a little burp.

I guess since she's decent now, I can take a closer look. When I reach the side of the rocking chair, Beth lifts the baby up, offering her to me. "Want to hold her?"

"Sure." Before I might have been leery of holding a newborn baby, but after Jake and Annie had their twins, I got over my reservations pretty quick. The key is, just don't drop them. I've held their kids plenty of times since, even changed diapers. "Mom told me her name is Ava."

As Beth nods, Shane says, "Ava Elizabeth."

"I picked Ava," Beth says. "Shane insisted on Elizabeth, after me."

"Ava McIntyre," I say. "It's got a nice ring to it." As I cradle the little bundle of joy in my arms, I gaze down at a cute little face with big blue eyes. I notice the brown peach fuzz on her head. "She looks like Shane."

My brother groans. "God, I hope not."

Cooper laughs. "I think he means she's got your coloring."

Luke jumps to his feet and runs over to me, wrapping his arms around one of my legs, trying to climb me like a little monkey. "Baby."

I reach down and pat his blond hair, which is short and spikey. "Yep. This is your baby sister. What do you think about that?"

Luke raises his hands. "Baby."

"You want to hold her?"

He jumps. "Baby."

"All right. Sit down."

Luke drops onto his butt on the carpet, and I lower myself beside him, careful not to lose my grip on Ava. I lay the baby across his lap and support her head and butt while Luke does his best to hold her.

"Careful," I tell him as he fidgets. "Be gentle."

Luke pulls her close to his chest and leans down to kiss her forehead.

"Can you say *Ava*?" I ask him.

"Baby."

"Close enough."

* * *

After quickly losing interest in holding his new sister, Luke gives her back to me so he can return to the train action. He climbs into Shane's lap. The kid has his thumb in his mouth as his other hand grips Shane's T-shirt like it's his blankie. As Luke leans back against his dad's chest, Shane drops a kiss on the top of his head.

I'm stoked for my brother. He has a wife he adores—literally, the girl can do no wrong as far as Shane's concerned. But that's fine, because my sister-in-law is pretty cool. And now he has two awesome little kids. I've never seen him so content.

Most of my siblings have found their soul mates—Shane, Sophie, Jamie, Jake, even my twin, Lia. And here's the shocker: Lia's engaged to her boyfriend. He once told me that getting the ring on her finger was the easy part. Getting her to agree to a wedding date was turning out to be much harder.

Only Hannah and I are still solidly single. I'm not surprised that Hannah is. She's a bit of a loner. She spends most of her time traipsing the mountains surrounding the small Colorado town where she lives. She seems happy, though, which is what matters. To each his own, or in this case *her* own. As for me, I'm a pretty social guy. I do a fair bit of dating; I just haven't found the right girl. Sometimes I don't think I ever will.

Most of the girls I meet, at least the ones close to my own age, just don't seem very serious. A lot of them are still in college, still searching for their path in life. They're mostly interested in partying, which isn't really my thing. I'd be more interested in a girl who knows what she wants out of life and is driven to accomplish her goals, whatever they are.

"When does Hannah's flight get in?" I ask.

Shane consults his watch. "Her plane touches down at O'Hare in about thirty minutes."

"Who's picking her up from the airport?" I'd offer to do it, but there's no way I could get there in time.

"Killian."

"Killian?" *That sly dog.*

"He offered, and I gratefully took him up on it."

I don't think it's any secret in this family that Killian Devereaux, one of Shane's security employees, has a thing for my middle sister. Everyone seems to know this except Hannah. "Are you by any chance playing matchmaker?"

Shane gives me one of his enigmatic grins. "I have no idea what you're talking about."

I hear some commotion coming from downstairs, so I figure the others are starting to arrive. I head down to see who's here and find a packed foyer. My parents have just arrived, along with Beth's mom. Jake and Annie are here with their three kids, and Jamie and Molly are just pulling in. Lia and Jonah are right behind him. Almost the whole family.

Aiden is clutching his stuffed stegosaurus, Stevie, which goes everywhere with him. "Hi, Uncle Liam." He smiles, flashing a pair of dimples. "Do you want to play cars with me?"

The guys are bringing in luggage while the girls take the kids into the great room.

"Sure, but after dinner, okay?" I glance at my brother Jamie, who's juggling a suitcase and two smaller bags. "Need any help, Jamie?" The guy's blind, but you'd never guess it. I don't think anything holds him back.

"Nah, I'm fine," he says as he carries the luggage up the stairs. "But thanks."

He's not even holding the railings. *Show-off.*

"When's Hannah getting in?" My brother Jake asks as he collects his family's bags, clearly intending to haul all of it upstairs in one trip. It looks like they packed for a month-long getaway.

"Pretty soon," I answer. "Killian's meeting her at the airport."

Jake laughs. "That should be fun."

7

Hannah McIntyre

I stare out my airplane window as we circle O'Hare International Airport. Good old Chicago—place of my birth and home to my entire family. But it's no longer *my* home. I moved away to go to college the summer after I graduated high school.

Down below, the streets are jam-packed with cars waiting in line for the arrival and departure zones. There are people everywhere—so many people. There are more people in this one square mile than there are within fifty miles of the small Colorado town I now call home.

I lean back in my seat and close my eyes, hoping I can meditate myself out of a panic attack.

Just breathe.

It's only for a weekend.

You can survive a few days of peopling.

The only reason I ever come back to Chicago is for family get-togethers—this time we're celebrating the birth of Shane and Beth's new baby. I hear they had a girl—Ava. That's a pretty name.

I try to get back to Chicago two to three times a year to see my family. I always come home for Christmas, and then at least once in the summer. And for the arrival of new babies and weddings. I came home when Luke was born and when Jake and Annie had their twins. My sister Sophie is due to have her first baby this spring, so I'll be coming back for that, too.

It looks like my sibs have been working overtime lately in the baby-making department. The upside to that is my parents are thrilled, especially my mom. She loves babies.

Nearly all of my siblings are either married, engaged, or practically engaged. Liam and I are the only holdouts, unless he's gone and gotten himself a girlfriend since the last time I saw him. I doubt it, though. I think he would have told me if he had.

The captain comes on and tells us to prepare for landing. I stow my carry-on bag and put my tray upright. I love flying—takeoffs and landings are my favorite part. I love the rush of the plane, knowing how fast it's actually going as it slices through the air. I get such an adrenaline rush.

We land smoothly and wait for what feels like forever to be let off the plane. I brought with me one carry-on bag and a backpack in lieu of a purse, and that's it. I'm a minimalist at heart, and this way I don't have to bother with baggage claim.

Eager to see my family, I march through the airport, the heels of my well-worn boots striking the polished floors. It's quite a hike to the arrivals lounge, where one of my sibs will meet me. As I step through the checkpoint, I pause and scan the crowded waiting room, looking for a familiar face. I spot one immediately—it's not hard, as he stands head and shoulders above most everyone in the crowd.

But he isn't any of the ones I was expecting. My heart stops as I catch my breath.

Killian Devereaux.

When our gazes meet, he tips his head in greeting and heads toward me. I'm relatively tall for a girl—five-foot-nine—but next to Killian, I feel small. He's got to be over six feet tall with big muscles, a big chest, and big shoulders.

And damn, those thighs.

"What the fuck are you doing here?" I ask him, before I can censor myself.

But he's not in the least offended. Instead, he grins. "Well, hello to you, too, *cher. Ca va?*"

Killian was born and raised in the Louisiana bayou. He says his family can trace their roots all the way back to Acadia—Nova Scotia—when the British kicked the French out. He once told me he was the first in his family to leave the area when he joined the Army right out of high school. His parents, siblings, and grandparents still live in Louisiana.

He's been out of the bayou for over a decade now, but he still has the accent. It's subtle, but French words slip into his vocabulary from time to time.

I took French in high school and college. I know enough to get by with the basics. "I'm fine. Killian, but honestly, why are you here?" I don't mince words, and I don't play games. It's just not my style.

The corners of his mouth curve up. "Shane sent me."

I'm going to kick my brother's ass. "If everyone was too busy to pick me up, I could have taken an Uber."

"Ouch." He winces. "You say that like I'm the last resort. Well, sorry, but you're stuck with me." He nods toward the exit. "I'm parked in the garage. Shall we?"

As I start walking, Killian reaches for the handle of my wheeled carry-on.

"Thanks, but I don't need any help," I tell him, moving out ahead. "In case you haven't noticed, I manage just fine on my own." I know I sound like a bitch, but I don't care. I hate to be patronized.

He follows a few paces behind me and mutters beneath his breath. "Don't I know it, *cher*."

The long walk through the airport gives me a few minutes to rein in my reaction to seeing Killian again. The last time I saw him was at Luke's first birthday party about three months ago.

Every time I come home, this guy shows up. It never fails. He violates my personal space with his stupidly handsome face—dark hair, dark eyes—and his muscular build that makes my belly quiver. And to add insult to injury, he starts talking in his stupid, sexy Cajun drawl—calling me *cher*—and it turns my insides to mush. All I can think about is getting naked with him.

And that sure as hell can't happen.

Ever.

I'm never moving back to Chicago, and I don't do long-distance relationships. So, we're fucked from the outset. It's not gonna happen.

"Slow down, *cher*," he calls after me. He chuckles. "Is there a fire I should know about?"

That just makes me walk faster.

I push through the automatic doors and head for the parking garage. He's right behind me the whole time, and I swear I catch the sound of his occasional laughter.

Once we reach the garage, I realize I have no idea where he parked, so I'm just walking blind, which is stupid. *I'm being stupid.*

Why do I let him affect me this way?

I stop walking so he can catch up.

"This way," he says, cupping my elbow and steering me to the right. "Ground floor."

His touch sends a shiver down my spine, a streak of electricity that lights a small fire deep in my core. My belly tightens.

I let him lead the way through row after row of cars until we finally stop at a black Jeep with tires caked in mud. The entire vehicle is in need of a wash.

Clearly, he's into off-roading. It figures. He's an adrenaline junkie, just like I am. It's one of many things we have in common—a fact I try to ignore.

"It's unlocked," Killian says, and he heads for the driver's door.

He doesn't offer to help me with my luggage, which I appreciate. After setting my bags on the floor of the rear seat, I open the front passenger door and climb in.

The inside is clean, yet utilitarian. Except for an open can of Redbull sitting in a cupholder and a CB radio mounted to the dash, the vehicle's empty. No trash on the floor. No empty cans or food wrappers. I like that.

His vehicle reminds me of my Jeep back home—a good off-road vehicle with all-terrain four-wheel drive and heavy-duty tires that can tackle the roughest of conditions.

Killian shoves a key into the ignition and starts the engine, which roars to life. "I sure wish I knew why I raise your hackles so much, *cher*."

He's right—I'm not very nice to him, and it's not fair. He's never done or said anything inappropriate to me. It's just my own reaction to him that makes me mad—at myself. I don't want to want him. I don't want to want anyone.

I shoot him a look but don't say anything. What can I say? *It's not you, it's me?* But as lame as that sounds, it's the truth.

He twists in his seat to watch behind us as he backs out of

the parking spot. Then we're off to Kenilworth. I crank down my window and let the wind ruffle my hair as I gather it up into a ponytail. It's a hot evening in September, humid as well. I'm used to the cooler temps up in the mountains.

I sit quietly and watch the familiar scenery zip by. Despite the fact that my heart is back in Colorado, Chicago is my first home. No matter what others might think, I do miss it. I just can't live here. It's too crowded, too confining.

* * *

Killian doesn't say another word on the drive to Shane's property. That's good, as it lets me get lost in my own thoughts. I hope Scout's doing all right. I know I shouldn't worry. My friend Maggie and her two sons will take good care of him while I'm gone. She and her kids love that puppy as much as I do. I wish I could have brought him with me, but traveling on a plane with a forty-pound Belgian Malinois puppy who is rambunctious as hell didn't seem like a good idea.

My gaze keeps drifting to the sight of Killian's hands on the leather-wrapped steering wheel. His fingers are long and tan. The backs of his hands are dusted with dark hair, and I watch the tendons flexing beneath his sun-kissed skin.

Damn.

Against my better judgment, I keep imagining what those hands would feel like on my body, touching me, brushing my skin, or cupping the ache I'm currently experiencing from just being around him.

Why does he have to be such a turn-on? It's everything about him—his looks, his manner, his confidence. Hell, even his accent is sexy. If I were looking for a guy—if I wanted that kind of complication in my life—this is exactly the one I'd want.

If I walked into Ruth Yellowhawk's tavern back home and saw Killian standing at the bar, I'd definitely give him a second look. But he's part of this world here—Chicago. He's part of my brother's world. So that means he's off-limits to me.

When we pull up to the house, Killian parks at the end of a long row of cars, trucks, and SUVs. He shuts off the engine and turns to face me.

Before he can say a word, I blurt out, "I'm sorry for being a bitch to you." The admission burns my tongue. "You don't deserve it." Then I open my door and hop out of the Jeep.

"Hannah, wait," he says as he jumps down from his seat.

But I ignore him, instead grabbing my stuff from the back and heading for the front steps of the house. I may be sorry for being a bitch to him, but that doesn't mean I'm going to let down my guard.

When I walk into the house, I glance back to see him leaning against the side of the Jeep, his big arms crossed over his broad chest. He's watching me with the single-mindedness of a mountain lion stalking its prey. As I close the door behind me, a shiver courses through me.

What I wouldn't give for a chance to tussle with that moun-

tain lion.

8

Beth McIntyre

After I coax a ladylike burp out of my daughter, she falls asleep in my arms. I continue rocking her while Luke plays contentedly with the train set. I can tell he's getting tired because he's sucking his thumb—it's a dead giveaway. He only does that when he's exhausted. And he's probably hungry. Dinner will be served soon.

Luke stands on Shane's lap and turns to face his daddy, his little arms going around Shane's neck.

"What's the matter, buddy?" Shane asks as he grips Luke's hips to steady him.

Pouting, Luke says, "Eat."

I swear, that child is always hungry. I guess it explains why he's growing like a weed.

Shane glances my way. "What time is dinner?"

"Elly said seven-thirty."

Shane checks his watch. "Another thirty minutes. I don't think Luke is going to last that long."

Sam rises to his feet. "I'll take him to the kitchen and get him something." He holds out his hands to Luke. "Come on, little man. Let's go get you some eat."

"Eat!" Eagerly, Luke vacates Shane's lap and runs to Sam, who scoops him up.

Cooper follows them out, leaving just the two of us with our new daughter.

Shane moves closer and crouches in front of the rocking chair. "How are you feeling?"

I reach out and run my fingers through his hair, smiling when he closes his eyes and leans into my touch. "I'm okay," I tell him. "Ava's quickly figuring out how to nurse."

"That's because she's a smart little girl." He gently brushes Ava's cheek with his finger. "Unreal. I can't believe we have two kids."

I laugh. "This is nothing. Your parents had seven."

"We've got a way to go to catch up."

Seven kids? Good lord, I hope he's not serious. "That's definitely something we need to discuss." I hand Ava to Shane so I can stand. "She needs a diaper change."

"I'll do it," he says as he carries her to the changing table. "Why don't you rest up before dinner?"

"Are you sure?"

He smiles. "I've got this. You go rest."

"All right. I do need to freshen up for dinner." And maybe I'll lie down for a few minutes. I'm exhausted.

* * *

I feel a gentle hand stroking my arm. "Beth? Sweetheart? Do you want to go down to dinner?"

My eyes pop open with a start.

Shane's sitting on the side of our bed, Ava tucked into the crook of his arm. "You dozed off."

I run my fingers through my tangled hair, trying to finger comb the tangles. "I meant to lie down for a few minutes, not fall asleep."

"You need the rest. I hated to wake you, but you should eat something. If you don't feel like going downstairs, I can bring you up a tray."

"No, I'll go downstairs." As I sit up, an unexpected wave of dizziness hits me. Wow, I could use a good straight eight hours of sleep, which I am not likely to get. I didn't sleep well in the hospital last night. And unfortunately, with a newborn to take care of, that's not going to happen anytime soon.

Shane sits in a chair near the balcony doors, holding our

daughter while I freshen up in the bathroom. When I come out, I join him near the glass doors and look out toward the lake.

Shane wraps his arm around my hips and pulls me close. "You feeling okay?"

"Yes." I gather my hair off my neck and hold it up for a few seconds. "Just warm. Is it hot in here?"

He shakes his head. "Not really. Let's go downstairs. You'll feel better when you've eaten and had something cold to drink."

We take the elevator down to the ground floor and head for the dining room. All of our family and friends are packed like sardines around a long table. There are nearly two dozen people here.

When Luke sees us, he squeals with glee. He looks quite happy perched on Cooper's lap, holding a little plastic cup of cut-up fruit.

We're greeted by a lot of cheering voices.

"Hi, everyone," I say as Shane pulls out a chair for me. I sit gingerly, as I'm still pretty sore.

Luke slips off Cooper's lap and comes straight to me. I lift him up and sit him on my lap.

"Mama," he says, smiling as he leans into me. He reaches up and grasps a strand of my hair. Then he leans his head back against me and makes himself comfortable as he shoves his thumb into his mouth.

"Somebody's tired," Shane observes with a laugh.

It's wonderful seeing everyone at this big table. Shane hands Ava to my mom, who's seated beside me, so he can go fill our plates at the buffet table. Since there are so many of us here, it's more practical to have a buffet line.

As Aiden approaches to give me a hug, he glances over at his new baby cousin. "I was hoping it would be a boy," he says, glancing up at me rather apologetically. "Now the girls are winning."

I bite back a smile. "Maybe Aunt Sophie will have a boy, and then you'll be tied."

Aiden looks at Sophie. "Did you hear that, Aunt Sophie? Can you have a boy, please?"

Dominic splays his big hand over Sophie's belly. "I'm afraid that's out of our hands, pal." And then he leans over and kisses Sophie's cheek.

Aiden doesn't seem convinced. "Why not?"

Everyone laughs.

"It just doesn't work that way, Aiden," Sophie says. "Sorry."

"Hey, don't look at me," Jake says, raising his hands in surrender. "He's way too young for *the talk*."

After Shane brings me a plate, I eat one-handed. Luke has fallen asleep on my lap, and I've got one arm wrapped securely around him so he doesn't spill onto the floor. Shane offers to take him from me, but I decline. I don't want Luke to feel like he has less of my time just because he has to share me with a sibling now.

Shane's sister Hannah comes up to say hello and give me a hug. "Congratulations," she says. "You guys sure do make pretty babies."

I squeeze Hannah's hand. "Thank you for coming. We really appreciate it."

Shane gets up to go refill his coffee. As he passes Hannah, he reaches out to muss her hair. "It's not the same when you're not here."

Of all Shane's siblings, Hannah is the most mysterious to me as we don't see her a lot. She lives halfway across the country. She makes it a priority to come back to Chicago for special events, but I haven't really been able to spend a lot of time with her. One thing I do know is that she's happiest out in the wilderness, and she absolutely hates the city.

Laughing, Hannah ducks out from beneath Shane's hand. "I missed you, too, big brother."

I scan the table and notice that Bridget and Calum look very content. I imagine they're just glad to have all their kids under one roof for a change.

Then I notice Killian Devereaux, who's sitting at the far end of the table on a chair crammed between Jake and Charlotte—his team. Killian's gaze follows Hannah as she returns to her seat next to Lia.

"Here, Beth, let me hold the little guy," Calum says as he reaches for Luke. "You need both hands free to eat your dinner."

When I happen to catch Hannah sneaking a look Killian's way, I start to wonder if maybe she's not as oblivious to his interest as she appears.

9

Killian Devereaux

It's fucking killing me to sit here watching Hannah from across the room. She smiles and chats with her family, acting like she doesn't have a care in the world. I think we both know that's not true.

When she smiles, her face lights up, and it's like a sucker punch to my gut. But then she'll glance my way, almost as if it's an involuntary action, and her smile fades, leaving her looking a bit lost and confused.

For some reason, I rattle that girl, and she hates me for it.

At least she was honest with me out in the Jeep. She's the

one with the problem, not me. I'd hang the damn moon for her, if only she'd let me. I admire courage and strength, and that girl's got both in spades. Too bad she won't give me a chance.

Bridget and Calum McIntyre bred three strong women—Sophie, Hannah, and Lia. I know Lia's tough as nails. I suspect Sophie is too, in her own sophisticated way; she has to be if she wants to go toe-to-toe with big Dominic Zaretti and hold her own. But Hannah? Deep down, I suspect she's the toughest of them all. It takes guts to leave her family—leave home—and go her own way. It takes courage and conviction. I get it. I respect it. Hell, I respect *her*.

I pretend to pay attention to the conversations swirling around me, but in truth, I'm watching Hannah out of the corner of my eye. I love seeing her laugh. I love her smile. I love the way she carries herself—a strong, independent young woman who's not afraid of anything. Brown hair, the color of dark chocolate, thick and wavy, hangs to her shoulders. Sometimes, like today, she has it pulled back in a ponytail. I'd give anything to be able to skim my fingers across the back of her neck, to feel her shiver. Her brown eyes are sharp and intelligent, and she doesn't miss a thing. Her smile is enough to make me beg. Yeah, I'd beg her if I thought it would do a damn bit of good.

Why am I so captivated by her? Why not some other girl? Because she's fierce—a she-wolf. She'd protect her own pack somethin' fierce. And she loves the wilderness, which makes me admire her even more.

I grew up in the Louisiana bayou, huntin' gators and Eastern

Diamondbacks. I doubt a rattlesnake would even faze her. Or a Bobcat. Or a mountain lion.

She's a girl after my own heart.

And she doesn't want a damn thing to do with me.

* * *

After everyone's done eatin', and lots of coffee, wine, and beer have been drunk by the grown-ups, the little kids wander off with some of the ladies and the grandparents to the great room. Shane and Beth take their kids upstairs to put them to bed. Jamie and Molly decide to walk down to the lake. Hannah disappears with her youngest sister.

That leaves just me and Jonah Locke at the table. He and I have a lot in common. We're both trying to rope a McIntyre filly, and that's not an easy thing to do. Props to Dominic for making it look easy. He's already married to Sophie, and they've got a bun in the oven to show for it.

"What'd you do this time?" Jonah asks me. He knows the score. We've talked.

I shrug. "I had the gall to pick her up from the airport."

Jonah laughs. "That's presumptuous of you."

"Yeah. It don't take much to set Hannah off. Not if I'm the one doin' it."

"Well, if it makes you feel any better, I'm not fairing much better with Lia. I managed to get a ring on her finger and a promise out of her, but trying to get her to set a date hasn't been easy. She doesn't want to talk about it."

"What is it with these McIntyre girls?"

"I think they're so independent that it's hard for them to consider letting someone in close. It's like men are their kryptonite." Jonah pats me on the back. "Don't give up. That's my motto. I've gotten this far, and I plan to keep at it until she finally relents and says *I do*."

"Why haven't you two set a date? She already said yes, right?"

Jonah nods. "She did. But she hates the idea of a *wedding*. She's averse to the idea of wearing a wedding dress, of all the pomp and circumstance. The hoopla. It's too much for her." Jonah's expression grows serious. "She doesn't like the attention."

"Then go get married by the justice of the peace. That's what Sophie and Dominic did."

"We might have to. But I really want her family to be there if at all possible. Calum and Bridget would hate to miss seeing their youngest daughter get married."

I get up and walk around the table, clapping Jonah on the shoulder as I pass him on my way to the door. "You're a good man, Jonah. You'll make her a good husband."

I hear laughter coming from the great room, but instead of joining them, I turn the other direction and find myself alone in the foyer. I feel like a fifth wheel here. Maybe I should say my goodbyes and head back to Chicago. It was a mistake coming here.

I'm about to do that when Aiden comes down the stairs with

a handful of Hot Wheels in his hands. His well-loved stuffed dinosaur, Stevie, is tucked securely under his arm. "Oh, hey, Killian." He stops to show me his little collection of cars. Peering up at me with big brown eyes, he says, "Do you wanna play with me?"

Another punch to the gut. There's a house full of people this kid could ask, all of whom would drop whatever they were doing to accommodate him, and he asks *me*. There's no way I can turn down an offer like that. "Sure, kid. I'll play cars with you."

After he hands me his cars, he takes my free hand and pulls me along with him into the great room. "Come on, Killian. Elly said she's gonna bring out pie."

* * *

It ends up being me, Aiden, Miguel Rodriguez, and Liam sitting on the floor playing with Aiden's cars. The grandmothers are sitting on one of the sofas holding Jake's twin girls. Calum, Jake, Dominic, Sophie, Cooper, and Sam are hanging out at the bar. There's no sign of Jamie and Molly, or Lia and Hannah, and I figure Beth and Shane are still upstairs with their kids.

Sure enough, Elly brings out warm pies fresh from the oven—not just one, but three varieties: apple, pecan, and cherry—as well as vanilla ice cream. Damn, I'm glad I stayed. Elly's cooking reminds me of home and my own *grandmere's* meals.

Before long, Shane comes back downstairs with Ava, who's wide awake. Apparently, Luke's out cold in his crib, and Beth is lying down to rest. Shane has a portable baby monitor clipped to his belt so he'll hear if Luke wakes up.

Beth's mom, Ingrid, calls dibs on the new baby, and everyone else has to wait their turn to hold Ava.

When Bridget McIntyre gets her turn, she looks around the room and asks, "Where are Hannah and Lia? They need to see this." Then she looks right at me. "Killian, honey, would you go find my girls and ask them to come here?"

I stand. "Yes, ma'am."

I'm not stupid. I know she asked me on purpose. I think the entire family is conspiring to get me and Hannah together. Too bad I'm not the one they need to be workin' on.

I have a good idea where I'll find them. I head downstairs to the lower level where all the entertainment can be found—the home theater, the pool, and the workout room.

I find the two youngest McIntyre daughters in the workout room—no surprise there. They're dressed in black boy shorts and black sports bras, both of them covered in a fine sheen of sweat.

For a few moments, I allow myself the luxury of standing at the viewing pane and watching them kick the shit out of each other. I've seen Lia spar plenty of times, but I've never seen Hannah on the mat.

Damn.

That girl can hold her own.

It's not only sexy, but it's reassuring too. I like knowing she can take care of herself.

What I wouldn't trade for an opportunity to wrestle with her on that mat. The idea of getting her beneath me—feeling her curves, her breasts, pressed against my body—putting my hands on her—my cock hardens at the thought.

Lia catches sight of me and pauses mid-kick. "We have company," she says to her sister as she nods my way.

Hannah pivots to the window, and a multitude of emotions flit across her face: shock, surprise, and finally annoyance. Her expression turns to a glare.

God damn it, girl. Give me a break, why don'cha?

"Don't blame me," I say as I walk into the workout room. "Your mama wants y'all to come upstairs and *ooh* and *ahh* over that new baby. And there's pie."

Lia heads for the changing room. "You should have led with the pie."

Hannah walks over to a bench and picks up her clothes. She looks everywhere but at me. "I'd better change, too," she murmurs.

"Hannah, wait."

She stops in her tracks and turns to face me.

"I just want to make it perfectly clear," I say, "that I have nothing but the utmost respect for you. I didn't want you to get the wrong idea."

She stares at me like I'm speakin' Chinese.

"I just wanted to say that," I add, feeling a little bit foolish now. "I didn't want you to think I was only after one thing."

Her expression softens, and for a split second, I glimpse a vulnerable side of her that I've never seen before.

"Killian," she says.

I know she's about to make excuses. "You don't need to say anything. I just wanted to be clear."

"Killian, it's not that I don't like you. I just *can't*. We live in two different worlds."

There's a tendril of hair hanging down her cheek—the rest of it's up in a messy bun. I reach out and tuck it behind her ear. "I don't understand why you won't give me a chance, but if that ever changes, I hope you'll let me know."

Before I further embarrass myself, I turn for the door. "Your mama wants you girls upstairs," I remind her.

And then I walk back the way I came, but instead of returning to the happy family celebration in the great room, I escape out the front door, cross the parking area, the yard, and take a much-needed walk into the woods to get my damn head on straight.

She said we live in two different worlds. Yeah, that's true. But I'm actually much more at home in her world than I am in the big glass and steel city. If she'd give me a chance, maybe she'd find that out.

10

Bridget McIntyre

I treasure moments like this... when Calum and I have our whole family with us under one roof—all our kids, their significant others, and grandkids.

Right now, Calum is hanging out with most of the boys at the bar. They're all laughing over something, and I can tell by the contented look on his face that he's just as happy as I am right now. No matter how big your kids get, they're still your kids. They always will be. It's bittersweet to watch them become adults, move out, and live their own lives. You're proud of them and their accomplishments, but you still miss those days when they were dependent on you for everything.

Right now, I've got my newest little grandbaby sleeping in my arms. Ava is as pretty as a baby can be. She has her mama's sweet face, but she has hints of her daddy's brown hair. That tickles me. I'd love to see a little female version of my Shane running around underfoot.

I notice Shane keeps looking over this way, as if he's checking to see that his baby girl is okay. None of these children lack for adults keeping an eye on them. They say it takes a village to raise a child. Well, I know all the members of this family will pull together to raise these kids and keep them safe.

Out of habit, I run through the birth order of my kids. Shane's at the bar with the rest of the boys, his dad, Cooper, Sam, Tyler, Ian, and Jonah. Sophie, who I suspect is feeling a bit tuckered out, is sitting on the other sofa with Molly and Annie. Jamie's at the bar with the guys, as is Jake. I have no idea where Liam is at the moment. That leaves my two youngest girls. God knows where they are or what trouble they're getting themselves into, but Killian promised me he'd find them and send them in here.

Sure enough, I hear a ruckus coming from the foyer—loud female voices. I glance over just as Hannah and Lia stroll into the great room. They're laughing as they tussle with each other, just like old times. Of all my kids, these are the two I worry most about.

I've never worried about my boys—well, except for Jamie when he got hurt in the military and lost his sight. I worried nonstop about him for a couple of years while he recuperated and tried to find his way in the world. Since then, he's proven over and over that he's a strong, resilient man who can accomplish anything he sets his mind to. Plus, now he has Molly in his life, and she's a fierce and loyal partner.

I never really worried about Sophie because she's as pigheaded as I am. I knew she'd never settle for less than she should—and marrying Dominic proved that. Despite some of his rough edges and his father's colorful background, he's turned out to be a fine husband for my eldest girl. And I know he'll be a good daddy to their baby.

But Lia and Hannah? Those girls have given me more than a few sleepless nights, I swear. Lia, because she's hard-headed and her own worst enemy. Thank god for Jonah. That man has the patience of a saint. Now if we can just get those two married, I'd worry less about her. I know she's wearing his ring, and she did agree to marry him at some point in the future... now they just need to make it happen.

Of all my kids, it's Hannah who worries me the most. My middle girl marches to the beat of her own drum, god love her. That's fine. I want all my kids to follow their hearts and be true to themselves. I just wish she didn't have to do that a thousand miles away from me.

Hannah's always hated the city. Growing up, she was her happiest when Calum and I took the kids camping in our old pop-up camper. That was a hoot. Fitting us and seven rambunctious kids in a camper designed to sleep five was a real challenge. But we made it work.

As the kids started getting older, some of them would bring tents, which they'd pitch beside our camper and sleep in. Namely Hannah, Lia, Jake, and Jamie—our more adventurous ones.

But by the time she hit high school, Hannah was pretty adamant that she was destined for the great outdoors. College took her to Denver, Colorado, and after that, she stayed for graduate school, and now she lives there working for a nonprofit wildlife organization. She lives in a small mountain town near the border of Colorado and Wyoming, and she spends most of her time on horseback in the mountains checking on wildlife populations—bears and wolves, mostly. And mountain lions. She looks for signs of illegal poaching and hunting operations.

It's dangerous work, especially for a young woman out there alone.

It scares me to death. It scares her dad, too. But neither one of us is about to rain on her parade. I don't want to be the type of parent who holds her kids back from following their dreams.

The girls stop in front of me and peer down at Ava.

Lia props her hands on her hips. "She sure sleeps a lot."

Across the room, Annie laughs. "All newborns sleep a lot."

"Can I hold her?" Hannah asks.

"Of course you can." I hand Ava over.

"Just don't drop her," Lia warns. And then she winks at Shane across the room.

Shane grins at Lia. "I'm pretty sure someone dropped you on your head when you were born," he says in retaliation.

"That explains so much," Jake says.

Lia glares at Jonah, who's standing next to Shane. "Are you hearing this? Aren't you going to defend me?"

Jonah laughs. "I'm pretty sure you can take care of yourself, tiger."

Lia laughs. "Good answer, pal. I forgive you."

Ah, it's good to have the kids together under one roof.

Hannah smiles down at the baby cradled in her arms. "She's so cute." She runs a gentle fingertip through Ava's hair and glances at her big brother. "She's got your hair, Shane."

"That's what I hear," Shane says, chuckling.

When I feel a pair of strong hands gripping my shoulders, I tilt my head back to see my husband standing behind me. Calum leans down and kisses my forehead. "We have some beautiful grandkids."

He tips his head to Ava, then over to the other sofa, where Annie and Molly are cuddling with Annie's twin girls, Emerly and Everly, both dark-haired, dark-eyed beauties like their mama.

I smile. "Yes, we do."

He grins. "That's because they get their looks from you."

As he says that, he slides his hands down my torso, his fingers grazing the sides of my breasts. My face heats up because, in a room full of highly observant people, I wouldn't be surprised if someone caught that.

Blushing—trying to act like my husband didn't just cop a feel in front of everyone—I turn my attention to Hannah, who's crooning to Ava. My heart contracts painfully. Hannah's a hard one for me to read. I just hope she's happy doing what she's doing. That's all I want for my kids—for them to be happy."

"My turn," Lia says as she takes the baby from Hannah.

Jonah comes over to stand beside Lia so he can get a better look at the baby.

"Don't get any wise ideas," she tells her fiancé. "We're just looking, that's all."

Hannah squeezes onto the sofa to sit beside me. "It's good to be home, mama," she says quietly as she wraps her arm around me. "I've missed you."

"I've missed you too, sweetheart."

More than she'll ever know.

Liam and Miguel come rushing into the great room, clearly excited about something.

"You guys have got to see this!" Liam says. He's doing something with his phone, and a minute later the massive flatscreen hanging on the wall comes alive.

A video plays on the screen, showing an arena with a boxing ring at its center, surrounded by a huge crowd of cheering people.

There's an emcee in the center of the ring, holding his microphone aloft. "In this corner, we have Jake McIntyre weighing in at two hundred forty-eight pounds."

Jake, wearing only a pair of black boxing shorts, moves into the center of the ring and raises his gloved hands into the air. The crowd roars enthusiastically.

"And in this corner, Ronald Jackson, weighing in at two hundred fifty-two pounds." Jackson does the same, and the crowd erupts in cheers.

"Oh, god, I can't watch this," Annie says, covering her eyes.

Aiden walks closer to the TV screen and cranes his neck so he can see the video. "Is that Daddy?" he asks, sounding rather dumbfounded as he points at the television screen. He looks to Jake, who is standing behind the bar popping the cap off a bottle of beer. "Daddy? Is that you?"

"Yep. That's me, buddy. A long time ago, before you were even born."

Aiden's mouth falls open. "Whoa."

After Jake left the military, he boxed professionally for a few years until he received an unfortunate series of concussions that ended his boxing career. Personally, I was relieved when he stopped boxing. I couldn't bear the thought of my son's body being battered. Of course, years later, Liam because a professional fighter and I had to face that torment all over again.

On the video, the match starts, and both men dance into the center of the ring, circling around each other as they vie for an advantage. Jake throws the first punch, hitting his opponent square in the jaw and snapping the man's head back.

Poor Annie is still covering her eyes. "Please turn that off. I can't bear to see him get hit."

Jake laughs from across the room. "Don't worry, baby. Spoiler. I won that match. I knocked Jackson out in the second round."

The video plays a couple of minutes longer. We can hear the

crowd cheering on their favorite fighters. It looks like a pretty even match, with both boxers taking their fair share of hits.

Aiden stares at the screen. When Jake takes a particularly hard punch to the face, going down for several seconds, Aiden runs to his father. It's not until Jake scoops Aiden up into his arms and hugs him do we realize that Aiden's crying.

"All right, turn it off," Jake says abruptly as he cups the back of Aiden's head with his hand. "It's okay, buddy," Jake tells him. "I'm fine."

I glare at my youngest son. "Liam, that's enough. Turn it off, please."

"That was an epic fight, bro," Liam says to Jake. "I think that was the fight that got me interested in boxing and martial arts."

Aiden struggles to speak through his tears. "That man hit you."

"He did," Jake says as he brushes Aiden's tears from his cheek. "But we were just boxing. I was okay."

Aiden's voice catches on a sob. "I didn't like that."

Jake glances across the room at Annie. "Your mommy didn't like it either. We won't watch any more of that, okay?"

"Okay." Aiden wraps his thin little arms around Jake's neck and leans in to kiss his adopted dad's cheek. "I'm sorry that man hit you."

My heart warms as I watch my son comfort his own son. It was a miracle that Jake and Annie found each other after having been separated years before, through no fault of their own. They were the victims of Annie's mother meddling in their relationship. But they got their second chance. I'm so proud of Jake for how he's welcomed Aiden into his life.

As Annie watches the interaction between Jake and Aiden, her eyes tear up. She rises to her feet, holding Everly on her hip. "Jake?"

He pauses to look her way. "Yeah, baby?"

"It's bedtime."

"For me, or for the kids?" He laughs at his own joke, as do all the other guys.

"I was thinking of the kids, but if you're ready for bed too, I'm sure that can be arranged."

Jake sets Aiden on his feet and wipes his hands on a bar towel. "See ya, fellas." He crosses the room and takes Emerly from Molly, lifting his baby girl high enough that he can blow raspberries on her belly. She grabs hold of Jake's dark hair and squeals in delight.

"All right, bedtime," Jake announces. He glances down at Aiden, who followed him over from the bar and is sticking close to his side. "Pick up your toys, buddy, and let's head upstairs."

After collecting his cars, Aiden makes a quick circuit around the room, hugging everyone. When he comes to me, he throws his arms around my neck. "Night, Grandma. I love you."

"I love you, too, sweetie." I kiss his forehead. "Sweet dreams."

"Good night, everyone," he says. "I'll see you in the morning."

Aiden smiles at the enthusiastic waves and "good nights" from his grandparents and aunts and uncles.

11

Annie McIntyre

It's nearly eight-thirty, and the girls are up way past their bedtime, and it's showing. They're both fussing and fidgeting, barely able to keep their eyes open. It's past Aiden's bedtime, too.

"Is it family time?" Aiden asks as we leave the great room and head for the stairs.

"You bet it is," Jake says.

It was Jake's idea to institute *family time* into our routine. Every evening, Jake and I get the kids ready, and then we all climb onto our big bed. Jake and I take turns reading to them.

This has become a sacred ritual for our family, and Aiden really benefits from it. It gives him the stability that he craves, and I know it's helped solidify his bond with Jake.

As we follow Jake up the stairs, the sight of him carrying our daughter Emerly sends a wave of emotion sweeping through me. I've loved this man since high school—since the day we met. It was a classic high school love story—the geeky teenage girl swept off her feet by the very handsome high school quarterback.

Jake was my first love, my first kiss, my first crush. And after a tragic parting, we somehow managed to find our way back to each other years later. We got a second chance, born out of an abusive first marriage on my part. Destiny had other plans for us; in the end, nothing could keep us apart.

When we reach our room, Jake opens the door wide for us, and we all file into the room.

"It's family time!" Aiden yells gleefully as he rushes into the room and climbs up onto our big bed.

Towering over me, Jake looks at me with a heated gaze. The look in his eyes tells me he feels it too. Fate gave us this second chance—it's a gift.

"Thank you," he says, and then he drops a sweet kiss on my lips.

He says this a lot to me—it means *thank you for giving me a family.*

Once in our suite—we now have an adjoining room for the kids—I take Evvy from Jake. "I'll get the girls ready for bed," I tell him, "while you get Aiden ready."

Jake takes our son to the bathroom to supervise getting him ready for bed.

While Evvy waits in her crib, I change Emerly's diaper and dress her in a clean sleeper. When I leave the nursery with the girls, Jake and Aiden come out of the bathroom, both ready for bed. Aiden's wearing his favorite pair of dinosaur pajamas, and Jake has changed into a pair of gray sweats and a black muscle shirt.

I allow myself a moment to admire the fine picture my husband makes.

Jake scoops Aiden up into his arms and gently tosses him onto our bed. The girls and I join them.

There's a small stack of children's books on the nightstand. Aiden grabs the one on top—his favorite, *Goodnight Moon*. "This one first," he says.

Jake and I sit propped up against pillows at the headboard with Aiden between us. While Jake reads the book, I take turns nursing the girls. They're mostly weaned, but they still want their bedtime feeding. Aiden has Stevie, his dinosaur, tucked close to his chest.

As Jake reads, Aiden clutches Jake's T-shirt, just to be connected to him.

Seeing the way Aiden trusts Jake makes my heart swell with emotion. Aiden's birth father, Ted, was an abusive monster who beat me. When Ted first began to turn his anger on Aiden, that was the final straw—I knew then that I had to leave him.

I couldn't let him hurt our young son. Thank goodness Aiden didn't let his early years with a bitter, angry father prevent him from forming a strong attachment to Jake.

As I gaze at my little family, my throat tightens. It scares me to think of how close I came to missing all of this. If Jake hadn't come back into our lives when he did—if he hadn't saved me from my abusive ex—I never would have known this happiness.

Jake reaches over to squeeze my arm gently. "You okay?"

I nod with a sniff. "Just happy. And grateful."

He smiles with a depth of understanding that can't be measured. "Yeah, me too."

Jake finishes the first book and goes on to read another one about frogs. By the time he's done with the second book, the girls are asleep in my arms, and Aiden can barely keep his eyes open.

"I think it's bedtime," Jake says quietly as he sets the storybook aside. He gets out of bed, picks up Aiden, and carries him into the adjoining room. A moment later, he returns and takes Emerly from me.

Jake and I put the girls in their cribs, turn out the light, and after making sure the baby monitor is on, we close their door and step back into our bedroom.

Jake slips his arms around my waist and draws me back against his muscular chest. "Have I told you lately that I love you?"

I chuckle. "Yes, just this morning."

Seemingly satisfied, he nods. He scoops me up in his strong

arms and carries me to our bed, lays me down, and then joins me. He leans close and kisses me, his mouth hot and hungry as his hand slips underneath my top.

I laugh when his hand starts traveling. "The kids just went to bed. The odds of one of them waking up and calling for us in the next five minutes is pretty good."

He chuckles softly. "Five minutes is all I need."

I lightly smack his shoulder. "You'd never be satisfied with five minutes."

"True."

Then he rolls us so that I'm beneath him. He wedges a muscular thigh between my legs and presses into me so that I can feel the ridge of his erection. Then he starts sucking on the skin at the base of my throat.

"Stop that." I lightly swat his rock-hard bicep. "You'll give me a hickey."

"So?"

"Your parents will see it."

"What, you think my mom's never had a hickey before? Trust me, she has. When we'd ask her about them, she called them *love spots*. Wear a scarf."

I laugh. "They'll know why I'm wearing a scarf."

"So? We're married, Annie. They know we fool around."

He slips his hand down my torso to the tingling spot between my legs and presses against my heated core. "Just a quick one," he murmurs close to my ear. "We'll take our time later tonight."

Twice in one night? The man's a beast. "Okay."

He starts unbuttoning my blouse.

The baby monitor crackles, and then we hear, "Daddy? I'm thirsty. Can I have a drink of water?"

With a resigned sigh, Jake pats my belly. "I'll be right back. Don't you dare move while I'm gone." He drops his forehead to mine and sighs. "Parenting is so hard."

* * *

One drink of water turns into Jake reading Aiden two more stories. I stand in the open doorway between the two rooms and watch them lying on Aiden's bed, a contented smile on my face.

After the second story, Aiden is asleep. Jake stays with him a little while longer, rubbing Aiden's back until he's sure he's sound asleep.

When Jake finally returns to our room, he quietly pulls the door shut. "He's asleep."

"Come here," I say as I grab his T-shirt and pull him close.

He walks me backward until we meet the bed. "Let's give them an hour," he says. "If they're all still asleep by then, I think we're good."

He's such a good dad.

12

Philip Underwood

Standing on the front steps of Shane's country house, my fist poised to knock on the door, part of me is wondering if I shouldn't get back into my truck, turn around, and head back to the city.

I have no idea if *she's* going to be here.

I know her dad's here, and his girlfriend, Erin. But I figure the odds are fifty-fifty that Mack's daughter—Haley Donovan—is here with them.

Fuck.

Part of me wants to walk through these doors and find out.

Part of me doesn't. Because being around her is nothing short of agony.

Mack's warning keeps looping in my head: "Stay away from my daughter, Phil. She's too young for you. I won't tell you again. Next time, we'll have a problem. Is that clear?"

"Yes, sir."

As his dark eyes narrowed, he got right up in my face to make his point. "Do you want to have a problem with me?"

"No, sir."

Now, to be honest, I'm a tad bigger than Mack Donovan. Yeah, he's a big guy, but I'm bigger. I've got at least twenty pounds more muscle than he does. Still, he's Haley's father. I can't go behind his back. And I sure don't want to get her in trouble. I need him on my side, not against me.

"Can I help you, son?"

I turn to face a man standing behind me on the drive. He's tall and sturdy with a silver buzz cut and a gruff voice, dressed in a pair of dusty overalls. I swear, he came out of nowhere.

"Phil Underwood, sir. I'm here to see the new baby."

The old man gestures to the door. "Go on in and join the party."

"Thank you, sir." I open the door and walk into a spacious foyer that opens to the second floor. I know Shane is wealthy, but damn. This place is unreal.

It takes me a minute to get my bearings. There's a curved staircase to my left that leads up to the second floor, and an elevator to my right. *They have an elevator? Really?*

The old guy follows me in and points straight ahead down a long corridor that leads into a large room. I can hear voices.

"Right through there, son," he says. "Most everybody is in the great room. I'm afraid you missed dinner, but if you hurry, you can get some pie—if there's any left."

Smiling, I thank him and proceed in the direction of the voices. I pass a library to my left and a huge dining room to my right, then a door to the kitchen.

When I reach the great room, I pause at the entryway and do a little reconnaissance so I know what I'm getting myself into.

I recognize pretty much everyone here. Immediately, I spot Mack at the bar—he's hard to miss—but his back is to me so he hasn't seen me yet. His girlfriend, Erin, is seated on one of the sofas next to Sophie.

There's no sign of Haley. I guess I should be relieved, but actually I'm disappointed. I haven't seen her in weeks. The only time I have a chance of running into her is if we cross paths in the apartment building where her dad and I both live. She's probably forgotten all about me and moved on to one of the legions of boys at her high school who'd surely give their left nuts to date her.

I know I would.

My shoulders fall a bit as the tension seeps out of me and I start to relax.

"Philip, hi!" Erin says as she waves me over. "I'm so glad you came."

Nearly a dozen pairs of eyes turn my way as I head toward

Erin. They all seem friendly enough—well, except for one. Mack has definitely spotted me, and he doesn't look happy.

I walk up behind the sofa where Erin is sitting and gaze down at the new baby.

"Her name is Ava Elizabeth," Erin says with a huge grin on her face. "Isn't she precious?"

I nod. "She is." I nod to Shane, who's over at the bar with the other guys. "Congratulations, man."

"I wasn't expecting you to show up here tonight," Mack says as he joins us. His voice is arctic.

I'm not exactly sure why he sounds so hostile. I look around—Haley's not even here. I turn to face him head-on. *Show no fear.* "Shane invited me. I'm part of Jake's team now."

Mack's dark eyes narrow on me, and when I hear voices coming from the foyer, I realize why he's pissed that I'm here. A second later, three girls walk into the room—Lia and Hannah McIntyre, and none other than Haley Donovan.

As soon as I spot Haley, my breath catches.

Holy shit.

Haley Donovan in a bikini.

I've never seen so much of her before. She's got long, long legs and amazing curves. Her dark hair is pulled back in a ponytail, and her dark eyes are wide as she stares right at me. She's stunning. She's gorgeous.

"We're going swimming," Lia announces to the room at large. "Anybody want to come with?"

Liam says he's in. So does Jamie. Jonah says yes. So does Erin.

I stand frozen in place, my gaze locked on Haley, who's staring at me like a deer caught in headlights.

Look away, I tell myself. Quit staring for god's sake.

"Don't even think about it," Mack growls low in my ear. He's standing right behind me now.

Seemingly over her shock at seeing me here, Haley walks right up to me—apparently, she wants me dead. "Hey, Philip. There's an indoor pool downstairs. Come join us."

My palms start sweating, and I swallow hard. *Tell her no.* "Um, sorry, Haley, I can't. I didn't bring my swim trunks."

Her eyes glitter as she smiles. "That's okay. You don't need them."

I hear Mack clear his throat behind me. "Haley—"

She laughs. "Just kidding, Dad." Then to me, she says, "Don't you have some shorts you can wear? If not, I'm sure Jake or my dad can lend you a pair. You guys are about the same size."

My heart is pounding, and I can't believe I'm even considering her invitation. I must have a death wish. "Well, yeah. I brought a pair of workout shorts."

I'm a dead man.

Erin stands and slips her arm around Mack's waist. "Then it's settled. Come with us, Philip. It'll be fun."

* * *

I head outside to my truck to grab my rucksack. Liam shows

me where my assigned room is up on the second floor, and I stow my gear in the closet. After changing into a pair of knit workout shorts, I follow Liam down to the lower level.

This place is unbelievable. We pass a movie theatre and a workout room down here before we come to the pool room.

Good grief.

It's huge.

The girls are already in the water, laughing and splashing each other.

Haley swims up to the side of the pool and hangs on the edge, her chin propped on her arms. "I'm glad you came. I wasn't sure if you'd be here."

Her smile makes my belly clench and my cock stir—definitely not what I need right now. "I would have been here earlier, but I had to work late."

Her bare arms are sleek with a hint of biceps. Her long dark hair is wet, and her smile is radiant. I try not to look down at her cleavage, but my efforts are pretty lame. Her breasts are sweet, round globes that I have no business looking at. I don't know how in the hell I'm going to survive seeing her in a *bikini* without incriminating myself and possibly getting killed over it. My dick is already reacting.

"Come on in. The water's fine," she says, and then she kicks back from the wall and does a backstroke to the center of the pool where she joins the other girls.

Just as I'm about to dive in, I catch a glimpse of Erin coming out of the changing room wearing a blue floral one-piece swimsuit. Wherever she is, Mack won't be far away.

* * *

Once I'm in the pool, I synch up the drawstring of my shorts to prevent them from slipping. The last thing I need is to flash my junk in front of Haley. Word would get back to her dad, and he'd kill me for sure.

I'm attempting to keep a respectable distance from Haley so I don't look like I'm trying to monopolize her time or that I'm staring at her cleavage. But the farther away I move from her, the more she drifts in my direction. I don't want to hurt her feelings or make her think I'm not interested, because—damn—I am. But if word gets back to her dad that I was hovering over her in the pool, I'd have to deal with an irate co-worker. Or worse yet, if Mack came down here and saw me with her, he'd blow a gasket.

I'm damned if I do, and damned if I don't.

"Haley!" Lia yells her name from the far end of the pool, the deep end, where the diving boards are. She motions for Haley to come join her and Hannah.

With one last look at me, Haley swims down to the deep end of the pool and climbs out. I watch as the three girls talk for a moment, and then Lia points at the high dive. Hannah nods enthusiastically, Haley not so much.

Lia climbs the ladder to the top of the high dive and walks

out to the end of the board. She turns her back to the pool and then does a backward dive off the board, her body arcing perfectly as she falls. Lia hits the water like a knife, slicing cleanly through the surface.

Hannah's up next, and she runs the length of the board and does a cannonball into the water, sending a geyser of water spraying everywhere.

"Your turn, Haley," Lia calls from the edge of the pool, where she's treading water.

Haley doesn't look too sure of herself as she climbs the ladder up to the high dive platform. She walks out to the end of the board, bounces on her toes a couple of times, and then stares over the edge at the water far below.

"Jump, Haley!" Lia calls out.

As Haley hesitates, her gaze seeks me out. She looks scared. Before I can even ask her if she's okay, she pinches her nose closed and leaps into the air.

Her terrified scream as she drops sends a chill down my spine.

Her free arm flailing, Haley hits the water hard, sending a huge spray of water into the air. Promptly, she sinks to the bottom of the pool. On instinct, I walk closer to the deep end of the pool.

When she breeches the surface, she's coughing and gagging on water, floundering.

Shit!

I dive into the pool and swim right to her. The moment I

reach her, she throws her arms around my neck and continues coughing so hard she can't keep herself afloat.

"It's okay, Haley. I've got you." I roll her to her back and tow her to the side of the pool where a small crowd has gathered.

When we reach the edge, she grabs hold and rests her cheeks on her arms as she tries to catch her breath.

"Are you okay?" Lia asks as she crouches down in front of Haley.

Hannah's there, too, and now Liam and Erin.

Out of nowhere, Mack enters the picture. He reaches down to grab Haley under her arms and haul her out of the water. After checking her over briefly, he folds her into his arms. "Are you okay, honey?"

She coughs again. "Yeah." She sucks in a ragged breath. "I guess I swallowed too much water."

Mack looks down at me and says, "Get out of the pool."

Well, damn.

As they say, no good deed goes unpunished.

Erin wraps a towel around Haley's shoulders and walks her over to a chair and sits her down.

Mack tips his head, motioning for me to follow him. He walks several yards away, far enough that Haley won't overhear us.

"What part of stay away from my daughter do you not understand?" he asks me, his hands on his hips, his posture hostile.

"She was struggling in the water, Mack. What was I supposed to do? Leave her to fend for herself?"

He scowls. "No, of course not." He crosses his arms over his chest. He still looks far from happy as he glances over at his daughter, probably checking to be sure she's okay.

She seems fine. The other girls are fussing over her.

"Philip." He pauses a moment as if he's collecting his thoughts and deciding exactly how he wants to say something. "She's an impressionable young girl, and you—" Frowning, he pauses and motions toward me. "You are just the kind of guy to catch a young girl's eye and fill her head with fantasies. You get my drift?"

I think that's a backward compliment. "Yes, sir."

"Look, I don't want to be the asshole here, but you're too old for her, and it's never going to happen. She's still a minor. But if you keep giving her ideas, you're going to break her heart. Is that what you want?"

A lump forms in my throat as I shake my head. "Of course not."

Mack nods. "I didn't think so. It's fair to say we're on the same page then, isn't it?"

"Yeah." When I glance over at Haley, I see her smiling at something Lia said. *She's okay.*

Mack's hard gaze is still locked on me. "I think you should get dressed and go find somewhere else to be. Don't you?"

I nod. "Yes, sir." I turn and head for the exit.

I shouldn't have come.

13

Haley Donovan

After my stupid choking incident in the pool, I decide to dry off and change back into my clothes. Philip's gone. After my dad jumped down his throat for saving my life, Philip left the pool room. My heart sank as I watched him walk through the doors and disappear without a single glance back.

I love my dad, and I know he means well, but sometimes he's too protective. I think it's because he and my mom never married, so I never lived with my dad. My mom got pregnant with me when they were seniors in high school. She got sole custody from the very beginning, so my dad was always sort of on the periphery, having me over every other weekend and one evening a week for dinner. I think he tries to make up for that by being a protective father.

But honestly, it's a bit hypocritical, as he's thirty-five and Erin's only twenty-two. There are only six years between me and Philip. Well, technically six and a half. I won't be eighteen until February. And once I'm eighteen, my dad can't tell me who I can and can't date. I just have to wait six more months.

My dad gets into the pool with Erin, and while they're busy goofing around, I change and go in search of Philip. At the very least, I owe him an apology. I was the one who asked him to come swimming. I'm the one who swallowed a gallon of pool water when I jumped off the diving board. It's my fault Dad chased him off.

I go upstairs to the great room, but there's no sign of him. In fact, there's hardly anyone here now, just Mr. and Mrs. McIntyre, Mrs. Jamison, and Mrs. Peterson. They're sitting around drinking coffee.

"Are you looking for someone, honey?" Mrs. Peterson asks me. "I think your dad was heading downstairs to the pool."

"Actually, I'm looking for Philip. Have you seen him?"

She points to the glass doors. "He went outside, through those doors. If you hurry, I'm sure you'll catch up to him. He might have walked down to the beach."

I head out onto the back deck, but it's empty. "Philip?"

There's no answer.

I scan the rear lawn, but I don't see anyone. It's dark out now, so it's kind of hard to see beyond the deck, which is well lit with strings of fairy lights. Moonlight shines on the beach, and there's a lamp post lighting the boat dock.

I glimpse a large, dark figure moving on the dock. That has to be Philip.

I probably shouldn't be doing this, I think, as I jog down the path to the private beach. Thank goodness it's a cloudless night, and there's plenty of moonlight to light my way.

When I reach the beach, I turn right and head for the docks where a number of boats are moored. There's someone at the end of the dock, looking out at the water.

As I draw closer, I can tell it's Philip. And surely he can hear me approaching along the wooden dock.

Philip is dressed in jeans, a dark blue Chicago Cubs sweatshirt, and a pair of well-worn white running shoes. His hands are tucked into his front pockets.

"Hey," I say when I reach his side. I'm so nervous, my heart is pounding. Maybe he doesn't want to talk to me. Maybe he's pissed at me since it's my dad who's giving him a hard time. I'm sure he doesn't need that kind of drama in his life.

Standing beside him, I'm amazed by his size. I'm not petite by any stretch of the imagination, but compared to me, he's a giant. Just looking at him makes me feel things. "I'm sorry about what happened in the pool room."

He glances down at me. "You don't need to apologize. It's not your fault."

"My dad shouldn't have jumped on you like that. You were just trying to help me."

He shrugs his broad shoulders. "He's just trying to protect you, Haley. I get that. And I respect him for it. Honestly, it's fine."

"Thanks for what you did. I'd never jumped off the high dive before. I guess I wasn't prepared for the sensation of falling so far. It was a little unnerving."

He chuckles. "Then why did you jump?"

"Because Lia and Hannah did it without even thinking. I—I guess I thought if they can do it, I should be able to."

"Ah, peer pressure," he says with a laugh.

"Yeah, I guess so. It was stupid. I think I panicked a bit when I hit the water—I must have opened my mouth and swallowed half the pool. So, thanks."

He turns back to face the lake. "Anytime."

I feel like I'm intruding on his solitude. He probably came out here to get away from me—away from the drama. I know I should leave him alone. But there's one thing I want to do before I give up on him. "Philip?"

"Yeah?"

"There's something I've been wanting to ask you."

He's silent for a moment, as if he's not sure he wants to know what it is. "What's that?"

"Next month is my school's homecoming dance. I was wondering if maybe you'd want to go with me." As soon as I say the words, I want to kick myself. He's been out of high school for years. I'm sure the last thing he wants to do is go to a stupid school dance.

He sighs heavily. "Haley."

As he rocks on his heels, I figure he's trying to decide how to let me down.

I should have kept my big mouth shut. "Never mind. I shouldn't have asked you. I'm sorry."

When he turns to face me, I have to crane my neck to meet his gaze. He's *so* tall. And standing so close to him only accentuates his height and the incredible width of his shoulders.

"Did you play football in high school?" I ask him on impulse. If he did, he probably plowed through the opponent's defense.

He laughs. "I did."

"What position did you play?"

"Quarterback."

Of course he did. He was probably the most popular boy in his grade.

"Did you go to your own homecoming dance?" I ask him.

"Yeah, I went."

And then a thought occurs to me. "I don't suppose you were the homecoming king."

He shrugs. "It's not all it's cracked up to be. I was dating the head cheerleader at the time, and she had the student body wrapped around her finger. They only voted me king because she was queen." He looks at me thoughtfully. "Isn't there a boy at school you want to ask? Someone closer to your own age?"

Ouch. That stings. "You mean someone my dad won't have a

fit over?"

He laughs again. "Yeah."

"No. There's no one I'm interested in." *No one except for you.* That part goes unsaid, but I'm sure he's figured it out. "Forget I asked. It was stupid."

To my surprise, he reaches out and touches my cheek. "No, it wasn't stupid. And if I could, I'd most definitely say yes."

I take a step forward, unable to resist the pull I feel, but he takes two steps back, as if he has to keep a certain amount of distance between us.

"You can say yes if you want to," I whisper. "It's just a dance."

He winces. "Haley, it's not that simple. Your dad has made it abundantly clear that you're off-limits."

"But I'll be eighteen in a few months, and then he won't have a say."

"Not for five more months," he clarifies.

It gives me a little thrill to know that he knows when my birthday is. I'm so frustrated I could scream. I've never known anyone like Philip—someone so handsome, so physically powerful, and at the same time so kind and considerate. I'm so tired of high school boys and their annoying immaturity, grabby hands, and sloppy attempts at kissing.

"It's not fair," I say. "You'd never take advantage of me. My dad should realize that."

"I'm sure he knows I'd never *mean* to do anything inappropriate with you. But he's also a guy. He knows that sometimes things happen. Sometimes things get out of control, especially when someone wants someone else so badly."

Is it that obvious I'm mooning over him?

My cheeks are burning. "You're talking about me."

He shakes his head. "No, actually I'm talking about *me*."

I can barely breathe. *Did he just admit that he wants me too?*

He reaches for my hand and links our fingers together. "I wish I could say yes, Haley. I would in a heartbeat if I could."

His hand is warm, his fingers long and strong. Just holding hands with him feels amazing—I can't even imagine what it would feel like to have his arms around me while we danced.

I take a step forward, and now we're just inches apart. As I suck in a shaky breath, I realize he's breathing hard, his broad chest rising and falling.

His other hand comes up to cup my face, and his fingers slip beneath my hair. I shiver at his touch and make a soft sound deep in my throat.

He mutters something under his breath—a curse, I think—and then he leans down, and he's staring at my mouth, and I think, *Oh, god, he's going to kiss me.*

My first real kiss.

I close my eyes, my heart thundering, and wait to feel his lips brush against mine... only they never do. When I open my eyes again, he's gazing down at me with a mix of heat and sadness in his dark eyes.

"Philip? It's okay if you want to kiss me."

He groans harshly as he pulls me against him, his arms locking around me as he holds me to his chest. I'm shocked by how hard he is—everything about him. His grip, his chest, even his, um... yeah. That's hard, too. God, I don't even know what to call it. *His penis? His dick? His package?* If I wasn't already blushing, I sure would be now.

His fingers slide into my hair, and he cups the back of my head and murmurs into my hair. "I'd give anything to kiss you right now."

"Then do it."

He chuckles. "I guess I'm my own cockblock." Then he slowly releases me and steps back a good foot. "Baby, if I started kissing you now, I don't think I'd be able to stop."

"Who's stopping you? I'm not."

He catches my hand and kisses the back of it. "*I'm* stopping me."

"I'm seventeen—"

"And I'm not. That's the problem." He glances up at the house. "I think you'd better go back inside before your dad comes looking for you."

"Are you afraid of him?"

His gaze hardens for a second. "No, Haley, I'm not afraid of your dad. I respect him because he's a good man and most especially because he's your dad. If I'm ever going to have a chance with you, I can't afford to make enemies with him."

A chance? He sounds like it's something he does want... at least one day. "You mean you want to?"

He smiles. "When you turn eighteen, ask me to take you to a dance. Wild horses couldn't keep me away."

When Philip holds out his hand to me, I lay mine in his. Then we walk back up to the house.

Elly greets us as soon as we step inside the great room. "There's a bit more pie left. Did you two kids have some?"

"Not yet, ma'am," Philip says. "Pie sounds great."

"Come on into the kitchen with me, and I'll get you some. Do you want ice cream, too?"

"Yes, ma'am," Philip says, looking down at me.

As Philip and I sit down at the little kitchen table to eat our pie, we keep sneaking glances at each other. Elly's too busy putting dirty dishes into the dishwasher to pay us any attention.

My dad comes storming into the kitchen. "Elly, have you seen—" He freezes in his tracks when he spots us. "Oh, there you are." His gaze goes to Philip, then back to me. "I just wanted to make sure you were all right after the incident in the pool."

"The young people are fine, dear," Elly says to my dad. She glances our way and gives us a small smile. "They're just having some pie."

"Well, that's all right then," my dad says. "Enjoy your pie."

After my dad leaves, Philip winks at me, and suddenly I'm even more in love with him than I was before.

14

Erin O'Connor

Mack returns to the pool room and drops down into the lounge chair next to mine.

"Did you find her?" I ask him as he settles into his seat, looking a bit preoccupied. "Is she all right?"

He nods. "I found her in the kitchen eating pie with Philip."

I laugh and reach for his hand. "See? I told you he's honorable. Philip would never take advantage of Haley."

Mack makes a scoffing sound. "He's a *guy*, Erin."

"So are *you*, and look at us."

"Yeah, but you're twenty-two, not seventeen. She's legally

still a child."

"Not for much longer. She's a senior in high school, Mack. She's a *young woman*, not a little girl."

He frowns. "She'll always be my little girl." He reaches for my hand and brings it to his mouth to kiss. "She's too young for—well, you know—grown-up activities."

I bite my lip to stop myself from laughing. He's serious. "Mack, um, girls are often doing grown-up things by her age. It's not unheard of."

Mack turns his dark eyes on me, clearly still unhappy. "He's too damn big for her."

I refrain from mentioning the obvious—that Mack is nearly just as big as Philip, and I'm rather petite. There's definitely a double-standard at play here. But he's her father—I get it. He's not thinking clearly.

Loud, raucous laughter draws our attention to the pool where several of the guys are roughhousing in the deep end. Liam and Miguel are ganging up on Jamie—two against one—while Dominic stands on the sidelines egging them on.

Mack shakes his head. "Idiots. They don't stand a chance."

I sit up straight in my chair and grab Mack's forearm. "What are they doing?"

"Trying to dunk Jamie."

Both Liam and Miguel are jumping on Jamie, pressing hard on his shoulders as they attempt to push him beneath the water.

Molly's watching from a lounge chair, laughing and yelling encouragement at Jamie. "Show them who's boss, baby!"

"That's not fair," I say. "Two against one. And Jamie's blind."

Mack laughs. "That doesn't matter."

Suddenly, Jamie disappears beneath the surface of the water. When he doesn't pop right back up, I start getting nervous. I shake Mack's arm. "Do something."

A moment later, Liam and Miguel both disappear beneath the water's surface. Truly alarmed now, I jump to my feet.

Dominic is laughing his head off, as is Sophie, who's lounging on a chair next to Molly. Molly looks completely unfazed.

"This isn't funny, guys!" I yell. "He could drown."

"Who?" Dominic says, still laughing. "Jamie? Hardly. Now as for Liam and Miguel…"

Just then, Liam and Miguel break the surface of the water, both of them gasping and red-faced. They swim to the side of the pool, where they hang on the edge.

When Jamie pops back up a moment later, he's waving two pairs of swim trunks in his hand. "You guys looking for something?"

Dominic's bent over, laughing so hard I'm afraid he's going to have a stroke.

Sophie whispers something to Molly, who nods as she laughs.

Jamie drops the two pairs of swim trunks in the water, letting them sink.

"You guys better start diving," Dominic says. "Unless you want to show the ladies your asses."

Jamie calmly resumes swimming laps as if nothing happened.

"He's a former SEAL, honey," Mack says as he pries my fingernails out of his arm. He's got tears in his eyes from laughing. "Rule of thumb: don't ever fuck with SEALs in the water. You're in their territory."

* * *

"You ready to go upstairs?" Mack asks me now that all the excitement has died down, and Liam and Miguel have managed to retrieve their swim trunks from the bottom of the pool.

"Yes." It's getting late, and I'm tired.

We've both already dried off after sitting on lounge chairs, so we don't bother to change before we head upstairs. I wrap my oversized beach towel around me, and we leave the others to their fun.

Once we reach the main floor, Mack leads us on a detour to the kitchen, presumably to check in on Haley. The kitchen is empty, so we try the great room. We spot Haley and Philip, along with Lia and Hannah, out on the back deck playing cards. They're laughing and drinking soft drinks.

"See, she's perfectly fine," I tell Mack. "And she has two very capable chaperones."

Reluctantly, Mack nods. Then he slides open the glass door. "Don't stay up too late, Haley."

Haley tries to hide her embarrassment. "Dad, please."

Undaunted, he wags a finger at her. "Remember, your room is right next to ours, so I'll hear what time you come to bed."

And then Mack glares at Philip, sending a message. *Alone.*

"Have fun, Haley," I say apologetically as I grab Mack's hand and pull him back so I can slide the door closed.

As we head upstairs, I say, "You need to lighten up on her, Mack. She's a good kid. You need to show her you trust her."

He makes a noncommittal sound. "Philip's not a bad guy," he says as we enter our room. "He's well liked at work, and he has a reputation for being highly competent at his job. It's just hard for me to think of my daughter with any man. Hell, I know what men like to do with women, and the idea of someone doing that with my baby girl—"

I drop my towel to the floor and turn Mack to face me. "You have to stop thinking about her like she's still a child. She's practically grown now."

Scowling, he nods. "I know. You're right." He looks away. "It's not easy."

He shoves his swim trunks off his hips and down his long, muscular legs. "I'm going to grab a quick shower. Be right back."

When he disappears into the bathroom, I get ready for bed, starting with brushing my teeth and then changing into my PJs—one of Mack's gigantic T-shirts, which I've adopted as my own. I get comfy on the bed with my iPad and check my work e-mail. While Beth has been on maternity leave, I'm acting manager of the bookstore. Kayla's taking over for me for a couple of days while I'm here. Fortunately, there have been no emergencies so far.

After a short while, the water shuts off in the bathroom, and

Mack comes out wearing nothing but a towel wrapped around his waist. His hair is combed, but still damp from his shower, and there are beads of water on his broad shoulders and chest.

As I take in the sight of his half-naked body, my chest tightens. He's so... much. Heat blooms in my body and my belly tightens.

He drops the towel and climbs into bed beside me, damp heat radiating off him. "Whatcha doing, babe?"

I glance down at my tablet. "I'm checking work e-mail."

"Everything good back at Clancy's?"

"Yes, fine."

He nods. "Kayla will do a fine job. You've trained her well."

I laugh. "Beth trained me well."

"Do you like filling in for Beth?"

"Sure. It's a lot of responsibility, but I enjoy it."

"If Beth should decide not to come back to work, do you think you'd like to take over officially as manager?"

My eyes widen in panic, and my pulse starts racing. "Do you think there's a chance she won't come back?"

He shrugs. "I don't know that for sure. I just think, with two little kids now, she might decide to stay home with them, at least for a while. Who knows? I'm sure if you ask Shane, he'd prefer that she stay home."

My stomach sinks at the thought of Beth not coming back to the bookstore. "But we have so much fun together at work. She can't stop coming."

Mack pulls me into his arms. "I didn't mean to upset you,

honey. I just thought it was a possibility."

I settle down and rest my head on his shoulder.

"Forget I said it," he says, and then he kisses my forehead.

"I'm sorry."

"I suppose you're right. It'll be harder for her to manage having two children at work, even with Lindsey there to help. Sam and I will help her too, of course."

As Mack runs his hand slowly up and down my back, his touch sends shivers down my spine. My body continues to heat, and suddenly I'm aching for more.

I skim my fingers across his chest, marveling at how well defined his muscles are. I press my nose against his skin and breathe in, loving the smell of his skin, which is still warm and damp from his shower. "Mack?"

"Hmm?" He dips his head to kiss me, his lips gentle as he seals our mouths together. Then his tongue slips inside my mouth, coaxing mine to play. He knows exactly how to make me quiver.

I exhale a long breath, followed by a moan.

His hands skim slowly down my torso, giving me plenty of time to decide. When he reaches my panties, he slips one hand inside them and cups one of my butt cheeks.

He smiles. "Do you want me?"

I return his smile. "Yes. You know I do."

But he always asks. He never takes anything for granted. Not after what happened to me. Not after what still haunts my nightmares.

Those dark thoughts return, unwelcome, and I draw inward on myself, trying not to dwell on the hazy partial memories that haunt me. I still don't remember what happened that night, but sometimes there are flashes of sight and sound that sneak up on me, sinking me into despair.

"Erin." His voice, low and gentle, pulls me back to the present. He catches my gaze and holds it. "It's just us here. You and me. No one else."

The rational part of my brain knows that the monster who attacked me isn't ever coming back. Mack made sure of it. The monster is *dead*. But the recollection of what he did to me is still here, hidden somewhere in the recesses of my mind. I can only hope and pray those memories never resurface. I couldn't bear to relive that horrific night.

He gently withdraws his teasing hand from the back of my panties and wraps his arms around me securely. He's my protector, both physically and emotionally.

I do my best to shake off the feelings of dread and despair that are creeping up on me. They strike at random times with little warning. But I don't want to live my life trapped in the past. I want to move forward, with Mack. "I'm okay," I tell him.

Still, his wandering hand doesn't return. I think I scared him off, or he's worried about me.

Trying to salvage the mood, I draw little circles on his chest, my finger skimming through his chest hair, over his nipples, and down to his ridged abs. I know my actions are having the desired effect because his chest is rising more strongly as his breathing deepens.

I can tell he's aroused—his erection is tenting the sheet that covers the lower halves of our bodies. He's hesitant to act on it, though. One of the other unfortunate outcomes of my assault is that Mack often feels like he's imposing on me when it comes to sex. As if a better man wouldn't ask for sex from a woman who was drugged, tortured, and raped.

But I don't want to be a victim. I want to be a strong, powerful woman who has a healthy sexual relationship with the man she loves. With the man who'd rather die than hurt her.

I replace my questing fingers with my mouth, trailing kisses across his chest and up to the strong column of his throat.

When a low, agonized groan escapes him, I smile.

I sit up and straddle his hips, knowing he wants to be *sure*.

"You're sure?" he asks as he slides his warm hands to the tops of my thighs. His thumbs brush against my skin, inching closer to the place where I ache for him.

I nod. And then to prove it, I grasp the hem of the T-shirt I'm wearing, lift it over my head, and toss it aside. My heart pounds mercilessly as his hungry gaze devours my naked body.

His hands come up, sliding up my torso until they come to my breasts. Smiling, he sits up and kisses me, his mouth gentle on mine. Gentle and seeking. My body continues to heat until I'm throbbing with need.

"Put me inside you," he says as he presses kisses to the side of my neck.

With a sigh, I sink down onto him and forget about dark

thoughts and painful memories. This is my present, here with Mack. This is all that matters.

15

Daniel Cooper

Just after midnight, I come across Shane in the kitchen, attempting to make a sandwich with one hand while cradling Ava in his other arm. "Here, let me help."

I take the baby from him and settle her in my arms. She's wide awake, squirming and stretching. I like the feel of her in my arms, the slight weight and the warmth of her. As I feel a tug on my heartstrings, I know this precious little one already owns a piece of my soul. Just like her mama and her brother do. They—along with Shane and the rest of the McIntyres—are the extended family I never had.

My family—my parents, that is—disowned me because of my sexuality. I was raised by an aunt, but she's gone now, god rest her soul. I wish she could have met Sam. I wish she could have seen how happy I am now, how utterly fulfilled.

As I stare down at Ava's sweet little face, so perfectly round with a tiny button nose and big blue eyes, my chest tightens. This little girl has a bright future ahead of her, because no matter what, her family will show her the unconditional love that all children deserve.

I gently stroke her soft hair. "You two sure make pretty babies."

Shane grins. "She's beautiful, but I might be a little biased. Right now, she's wide awake and keeping her mama up, when her mama should be sleeping."

Shane finishes assembling his plate for a midnight meal.

I nod toward the door. "You go on up. I'll bring Ava to you in a few minutes. I just need to wrangle Sam. He's on the back patio playing poker with the youngsters."

Leaving Shane to it, I head through the great room and out the back doors. Sure enough, the young guys—Sam, Philip, Liam, Ian, and Miguel—are gathered around a table playing cards. I'm glad to see Ian's fitting right in with the guys. "Howdy, boys."

As they're between hands, Sam jumps to his feet and takes the baby from me. "Hey, little princess," he says as he coos to her. He leans down to touch the tip of his nose to hers. "Uncle Sammy loves you."

Ian holds out his hands. "She wants Uncle Ian."

Liam shoots to his feet. "What about me?" He holds out his hands for his turn to hold the baby. "Uncle Liam here."

"You boys can fight over her in the morning," I say. "It's late. I'm supposed to take Ava up to Shane and Beth's room." I grip the back of Sam's neck. "And you're needed upstairs."

Sam grins at me, his face heating as the rest of the boys snicker at him. Ian gives him a wink.

Sam scoops his winnings off the table and pockets the change. "Sorry, guys, but you heard the man. I'm needed elsewhere. You'll have to get along without me."

Ignoring their teasing jests, Sam and I walk back into the great room and head upstairs.

"I can't stop looking at her," he says as he gazes down at Ava. "Have you ever seen anything so adorable? She definitely takes after Beth."

There's something about watching Sam fawning over a baby that hits me right in the gut. He loves kids. We've talked about having our own one day. But to be honest, it's hard for me to wrap my mind around it. I grew up ostracized. I thought I would never have a chance at a family. And now things are different, and that dream isn't quite so elusive anymore.

My throat tightens and I choke up when I think about how shitty my parents were. It was a generation ago, and things were a lot different back in the seventies when tragedy forced to come out as a teen. My parents kicked me out of the house, and that was it. They didn't want anything more to do with me.

I don't understand how a parent could do that to their own kid.

Sam cups my cheek, getting my attention. "Hey. Earth to Danny. Where'd you go? Come back here."

I shake myself mentally. "Sorry. I was thinking about my own parents. They weren't good role models."

"No, they weren't. But that's irrelevant because we'd be great parents, and that's what matters." Sam leans forward and kisses me, his lips brushing lightly against mine.

When we reach the door to Shane and Beth's suite, Sam pauses. His brown eyes glitter with emotion. "I want a child," he says quietly as he meets my gaze. "I want *us* to have a child. We'd make great dads."

I cup the back of his neck and pull him in for a kiss. "I know. Me too."

He smiles. "You'd be an amazing father."

A sharp pain pierces my chest. "You don't think I'm too old? I'm not a spring chicken, Sam. I don't even know if I'm eligible to adopt at my age. What's the cut-off?"

"I don't know, but it doesn't matter. We'll figure it out. There's always a way. We could consider surrogacy."

"You make it sound so easy."

Sam frowns. "I'm not saying it's easy. I just know if we both want it badly enough, we'll make it happen."

Heat swells in my chest. When I reach up to brush back his hair, I picture a little red-headed child, and the pang of longing I feel is sharp. I never thought I'd be fortunate enough to have Sam in my life, let alone the prospect of a child too.

I reach past Sam and knock quietly on Shane's door. A moment later, he opens the door. "Thanks, guys."

The bed is empty, and we can hear Beth speaking softly to Luke over the baby monitor. We follow Shane into the nursery and find Beth leaning over the side of his crib, rubbing Luke's back. When she sees us, she straightens and nods toward the door.

We all return to the bedroom.

"He's having trouble settling down tonight," she says quietly, as if she's afraid she'll wake him.

When Ava lets out a plaintive squawk, Beth reaches for her. "It's time for this little one to nurse." Then she makes herself comfortable in an upholstered armchair and proceeds to feed the baby.

"I'm so proud of you, kiddo," I tell her. I remember very clearly how she suffered from postpartum depression after Luke's birth. That was a dark time for all of us. I think we've all been secretly afraid it might happen again—especially Shane. I know he's tried to hide it, but her depression after Luke was born really scared him.

She smiles up at me, clearly happy, even if exhausted. "Thank you." She tosses her hair back from her face, laughing as she says, "Is it hot in here, or is it just me?"

I lay my hand on her shoulder and give her a reassuring squeeze. "Try to get some rest. You'll feel a lot better after you've had a good night's sleep."

I get a good look at her—she looks tired, which is to be expected. The poor girl just gave birth. But she also looks a bit flushed to me. "We'll leave you two alone," I say, catching both Sam's and Shane's gazes and nodding toward the door.

Shane steps out into the hallway with us and pulls the door closed behind him.

"How's she doing?" I ask.

"She's doing well. Really well, in fact. Ava's nursing fine. That's a huge relief. It was much more difficult in the beginning with Luke."

"She looks a bit flushed to me. Keep a close eye on her."

Shane nods. "Believe me, I will. She's probably already sick of me asking her how she's doing."

* * *

I reach for Sam's hand as we head for our suite. Once we're inside our room, I pull him into my arms, one hand cupping the back of his head as I draw him close for a kiss. Our mouths come together, hot and hungry. All day, I've been wantin' to get my hands on him, but it's been hard because we're in a house full of people.

I back him into the wall and hold him there, one hand grasping his chin as I hold him still for a kiss.

He grips my shoulders tightly, as if he needs something to hang on to.

I lean in close and whisper in Sam's ear. "I want you."

He presses his head back into the wall and groans. "God, yes. Please."

I slide my hands up beneath his T-shirt and stroke his lean chest. I splay my fingers over his pecs and massage his muscles. When his breathing picks up, I pull off his shirt. His beautiful chest is bare and heaving as he sucks in air. When I lean in to lick his nipple, he shivers.

I pin his wrists to the wall and lean in close. "Do you want me?"

His answer is a hot, rushed breath. "Yes."

I step closer to him, pressing my erection against his, aligning our flesh. Both of us are hard and throbbing. "Inside you?"

He nods.

I give him one last kiss before I release him, and he heads for the bathroom to get himself ready.

While I'm waiting, I pour myself a shot of whiskey and carry it out onto the balcony. My mind's preoccupied tonight with thoughts of marriage and babies. I want that for us, and I know Sam wants it too. There's no reason why we can't have what the others have. Since coming out, I've become far more comfortable with the idea.

I guess first things first. We need to get married. Shane said he'd get licensed to perform the ceremony for us—just like I did for him and Beth. We just need to pick the venue and a date.

When I hear a noise behind me, I glance back and see Sam standing at the balcony doors, naked and hard. His eyes are glittering with anticipation.

My pulse pounding, I knock back my shot of whiskey and walk inside.

16

Shane McIntyre

Watching my wife nurse our daughter is mesmerizing. A soft light from the chairside lamp casts a glow on her rounded breast. Her slender fingers cup her plump breast as she holds it for the baby, whose tiny mouth suckles vigorously.

Beth is a beautiful woman and far stronger than anyone realizes. And she's given me more than I ever dreamed possible.

She finishes nursing Ava and props the baby against her shoulder so she can burp her. I walk up next to her chair and run my fingers through Beth's hair, the silky blonde strands slipping through my fingers. "Is she finished?"

She nods. "I just need to change her diaper and put her in a clean sleeper."

"I'll do that while you go get ready for bed."

Smiling gratefully, she hands me our daughter.

I watch as Beth walks tiredly to the bathroom and disappears inside. While she's getting ready, I change Ava's diaper, tend to her umbilical cord, and dress her in a sleeper. Then I lay her in the bassinet beside our bed and turn down the light.

While Beth's getting ready for bed, I peek in on Luke to make sure he's still asleep. He's lying on his stomach with his knees drawn up and his little butt in the air, his thumb in his mouth. I reach down and pat his back. "You're a big brother now, buddy. That means you have a lot of responsibility coming your way. You need to watch out for your sister."

Just as I return to our room, Beth comes out of the bathroom dressed in a sheer white nightgown, her hair freshly brushed and lying loose on her shoulders. As always, she takes my breath away.

I help her into the bed and cover her with the sheet and comforter. "I'll be right back."

I make a quick trip to the bathroom to get ready for bed. As soon as I return and lie down, she turns to me with a sigh and lays her arm across my torso. "You're such a good dad," she says with a sleepy smile as she tucks her head in the crook of my shoulder.

When I brush her hair back, I notice that her forehead feels warm. "Do you feel all right, sweetheart?"

She snuggles closer. "Just tired." Then she winces and presses a hand to her abdomen. "I've been cramping a lot today, and I'm spotting, but I guess that's to be expected."

"I would think so. You gave birth just forty-eight hours ago. And you probably overdid it today. I think tomorrow you should rest in bed."

I roll her onto her belly so I can give her a back rub. I know she likes that. She deserves a little bit of pampering. She's had a hell of a day and hasn't complained once.

When she drifts off to sleep, I press my lips to her forehead. "Good night, sweetheart. Sleep well."

I lie awake for a while longer, just watching her sleep.

* * *

A quiet sound penetrates my sleep, waking me instantly. One of the residual benefits of having served in special ops is the ability to wake at the slightest sound.

I check the time—two o'clock in the morning. Lying quietly, I listen, trying to determine what it was that woke me. I focus on the baby monitor, which tells me Luke is sleeping soundly. I don't hear any noises coming from Ava's bassinet, just her soft breaths.

As I glance down at Beth, she rolls away from me, sighing heavily, then rolls right back. Then, with a soft moan, she kicks off her covers.

As soon as I press my palm to her forehead, instinct has me out of bed and searching in the bathroom cupboard for a digital thermometer. I find one of those infrared devices that I can simply swipe across her heated skin.

When the read-out glows red, my gut tightens as my suspicions are confirmed. She has a raging fever. One hundred and four degrees Fahrenheit.

Shit!

I shake her gently. "Beth? Sweetheart?"

She moans and turns away.

"Beth?"

I take her temperature again, just to be sure, and the outcome is the same. *Damn it.* She must have an infection, most likely something to do with the delivery.

I grab my phone and call Cooper.

Cooper answers promptly, his voice rough with sleep. "What's wrong, Shane?"

"Beth's temperature is a hundred and four. I'm taking her to the ER."

"Shit. Do you want me to call 911?"

"No. There's a hospital in Evanston. I can get her there faster myself. I need you and Sam to watch the kids. I don't want to wake anyone else at this hour until we know what's going on."

"We're on our way," Cooper says, and then he ends the call.

I throw on a pair of jeans and a T-shirt, socks and sneakers. Then I grab Beth's robe. There's no time for her to change.

I turn the lights on low, just enough illumination so I can see what I'm doing. When I hear a quiet knock on the door, I open it. Cooper and Sam are standing there, dressed in sweats and T-shirts, and clearly just out of bed.

"I'm sorry for getting you guys out of bed at this hour."

"Don't be ridiculous," Cooper says as they walk inside.

I point to the diaper bag on the floor beside the bassinet. "There's a cannister of powered formula in there, along with some bottles. You'll have to sterilize the bottles—"

Cooper lays his hand on my chest. "We know what to do. Go."

Sam is sitting on Beth's side of the bed, his palm on her forehead. "She's burning up."

While I throw a few basics into an overnight bag, Sam talks quietly to Beth.

"Hey, princess," he says. "You okay?"

She stirs with a whimper and finally opens her eyes. "Why is it so hot in here?" Her voice is slurred.

"You have a fever, sweetie," Sam says. "Hubby's taking you to the hospital."

She frowns. "No. I can't go. I can't leave my kids."

Sam brushes her hair back from her face. "Don't worry. Danny and I have everything covered. You go get checked out so you can come back soon."

Once I have our overnight bag packed, Sam sits Beth up while I slip her arms into the sleeves of her robe.

"No," she cries, trying to push me away. "I can't go." She

glances at Ava in her bassinet. "I can't leave her, Shane. She needs me. She needs to nurse."

Cooper crouches down in front of Beth. "Don't worry about the kids, honey. Sam and I will take good care of them. You need to go so the doctors can find out what's wrong."

"I can't," she murmurs, shaking her head adamantly. "I can't leave her." Then she starts quietly sobbing.

Cooper looks my way. "Go," he says as he heads for the door. "I'll pull the Escalade up to the front doors. Give me five minutes, and then you bring her down."

And then Cooper's out the door.

I look to Sam. "Take care of them."

He nods. "You don't need to worry about your kids. Just worry about your wife."

Despite her weak protests, I lift Beth into my arms and carry her out of our room, down the hall, and down the stairs to the foyer.

As I approach the front door, it opens. Cooper's standing there, breathing hard. He follows me outside and opens the front passenger door so I can deposit Beth on the seat and secure her seatbelt.

Cooper clutches my shoulder. "Call us as soon as you know anything, no matter the time."

"I will. Tell everyone in the morning. There's no use waking anyone else right now. They'll find out soon enough."

Then I climb into the driver's seat and head south to the nearest major hospital.

"Where are we going?" Beth asks as she gazes out her window at the dark, shapeless scenery.

"We're going to the hospital, honey."

"Why?"

"Because you're not well." I reach over to touch her forehead, which is, of course, still frighteningly hot. "You have a very high fever. You probably have an infection."

She starts crying. "I can't leave my baby."

It's all I can do to keep both hands on the steering wheel. "Ava will be all right, sweetheart. Sam and Cooper will take excellent care of her. You know they will."

"But I need to nurse her."

I reach for her hand and squeeze it. "They'll make formula for her until you get back home. Right now we have to find out what's wrong with you."

Twenty minutes later, I park in front of the emergency room at Evanston Hospital. I rush around to the front passenger door, open it, and lift Beth out of the vehicle. She's so weak, she can't even stand. A security guard near the front entrance sees us and directs someone to bring a wheelchair.

As I push her inside, it's clear she's delirious from the fever. She's mumbling incoherently and crying, obviously confused and panicking.

One of the hospital staff takes her straight back to the treatment area while I follow close behind.

As I run down her recent medical history, a nurse collects her vital information and obtains a blood sample.

"What are her symptoms?" the nurse asks me.

"You mean besides the fever? Earlier this evening, she complained of cramping and spotting."

Shortly after, a physician comes in to perform an examination. "Given her symptoms, and the fact that she recently gave birth," he says, "I suspect part of the placenta is still in her uterus. We'll go in and remove any tissue that was left behind. She'll need to be placed under general anesthetic."

"Is it a safe procedure?"

"Well, there's always some risk when a patient is under general anesthesia, but yes, it's considered a safe procedure."

"When are you going to do it?"

"As soon as you sign the paperwork and we get an obstetrician here. As her husband, you'll need to give permission."

I nod. "Of course."

"I'll send someone in to start the paperwork," the physician says, and then he walks out of the room.

Beth is lying in a hospital bed, flushed and restless. They're already giving her an IV of fluids with something to bring down her fever. I reach for her hand and cradle it in both of mine—even her hand is hot. Her entire body is on fire. I'm not sure she even understands where she is.

As I kiss her hand, I wish fervently that was just a bad dream, and that we were really back home with our kids.

"You need to get well and come home soon," I murmur under my breath as tears blur my vision. "Our kids need you." My throat tightens. "I need you."

Half an hour later, a nurse comes in. "We're going to prep her for the procedure now. I need to ask you to step out to the waiting room."

Reluctantly, I stand and gaze down at my wife. She's asleep and has no idea what's happening or why. I lean down and kiss her forehead, and then gently I press my lips to hers. "I'll be back by your side just as soon as I can." I squeeze her hand gently. "I won't be far from you, I promise."

With one last kiss, and a murmured "I love you," I walk out of her treatment room and head for the waiting room.

When I step through the doors, Cooper is there, looking as haggard as I feel.

"What are you doing here?" I ask him.

"Sam's with the kids. We figured you needed someone here with you. And frankly, I needed to be here, too. Not just for you, but for her." He nods toward a row of empty seats. "Have a seat, Shane, before you fall down."

I nod. Cooper is the closest thing Beth has to a father, since hers died when she was an infant. Cooper takes his adoptive role seriously. I'm grateful for that, because she needs him in her life. And he needs her too.

Cooper gets us each a coffee from the vending machine while I pace. I have to keep moving. My adrenaline is through the roof, and I can't sit still.

I'm torn in half. Of course I need to be here with Beth—no question about that—but part of me worries about our kids. If Luke wakes up in the middle of the night, and we're not there to comfort him, he'll be upset. I take solace in knowing that Sam is with him. Sam is family.

A nurse comes out to tell us that the procedure is underway. "I'll keep you posted."

So, now we wait. And I pace.

Cooper hands me my cup of black coffee. "She's going to be fine," he says in his gruff voice.

"I know."

"No, I mean it. You're pacing like a man on death's row. She's going to be fine. Now sit down and relax."

"I can't sit."

Two hours later, a nurse comes out to the waiting room. "Mr. McIntyre? Everything went well, and your wife is in recovery. You can come see her now."

"Was it the placenta?"

The nurse nods. "Yes. But don't worry. Dr. Mitchell says she'll be fine now."

I'm struck by an overwhelming sense of relief that they know what caused her fever. Now I just want to see her for myself and make sure she's all right.

17

Beth McIntyre

Disoriented and confused. That's all I feel right now as I fight to wake up. I'm so exhausted, I can barely open my eyes.

When I manage to look around me and take stock, I'm surprised to discover I'm in a hospital room. Shane is sitting beside my bed, leaning his head back against the wall, his eyes closed. I try to say his name, but what comes out is little more than a croak.

Still, it's enough to get his attention. He sits up straight, his eyes flashing open, instantly alert. "Sweetheart." He shoots out of the chair and sits carefully on the side of the bed and takes my hand in his. When he lays his other hand on my forehead, much of the tension in his posture evaporates.

"Why am I here?" I ask him.

He frowns. "You don't remember?"

I shake my head. "No. I don't remember anything."

"You woke up in the middle of the night with a high fever, and you were delirious. I brought you to the ER at Evanston Hospital. Turns out there was some placenta left in your uterus after Ava's birth. It was an infection causing the fever. The doctor removed it, and you're fine now." He touches my forehead once more as if to double-check. "The fever's gone."

"What time is it?"

Shane checks his watch. "Eight-thirty am."

I touch my breasts, which are swollen and painfully hard. "Shane, I need to nurse Ava soon. If I can't, I'll need to start pumping."

He nods. "I know. I'll take you home as soon as you're cleared to leave."

I look at the bandages on my arm, where an IV must have been. "Do you know what they gave me? Is it still okay for me to nurse?"

He nods. "Your doctor says you can continue to nurse Ava. It's okay."

"The kids are at Kenilworth?"

"Yes. Sam's with them. Cooper's here with us, out in the waiting room."

I'm sore all over, but my head is clearing. Right now, what I feel is an urgent need to be with my kids. "I want to go home, Shane. Please. I *need* to go home."

He stands. "I'll see what I can do."

Half an hour later, Shane manages to track down the obstetrician who performed my procedure. The doctor comes to my room to check on me. "You're responding well," he says. "Your vitals are normal. How do you feel?"

"Like I was hit by a train. Everything hurts."

He nods. "I'm afraid you'll be sore for a few days. Take warm baths and over-the-counter pain medicine if you need it to help manage the discomfort. I recommend you see your obstetrician in a week to follow up, or immediately if your fever returns."

* * *

While Shane deals with the discharge paperwork, Cooper waits with me in my room.

I'm dressed in an outfit Cooper brought with him. We're sitting together on a small sofa, and he puts his arm around me. "Please don't do that again."

I smile. "Do what?"

"Scare me like that."

"I'm sorry. It wasn't intentional."

When Shane returns to the room, he says I'm cleared for discharge. Cooper leaves us to bring the Escalade up to the main doors, and Shane helps me into the front passenger seat. Cooper follows us home in his own car.

As he drives us home, Shane reaches over to hold my hand. "I'm sure we have two kids who are eager to see you."

When we arrive back at the house, Shane hops out of the vehicle and opens my door. He helps me climb down and puts his arm around me as he walks me inside.

Elly, Bridget, and my mom are waiting for us in the foyer.

"How do you feel, honey?" Mom asks as she gives me a gentle hug.

I do my best to smile. "I'm okay." *Not really.* I hurt all over.

"Can I get you anything?" Elly asks. "Are you hungry? Thirsty?"

"Just let me get her upstairs and into bed first," Shane says as he leads me toward the elevator. "Right now, she needs rest."

I've never been so glad for this elevator. The idea of walking up that staircase is a little more than I can handle right now.

Slowly, we make our way down the upstairs corridor to our room. Shane opens the door.

Sam is sitting on the side of the bed with a crying baby in his arms, holding a bottle of formula. He glances up at us, clearly relieved.

"She took the first couple of bottles just fine, but she's not cooperating with this one."

I sit beside Sam and reach for Ava. I cradle her close and gently rock her in my arms. Her cries quiet quickly as she nuzzles my chest. "I'm here, baby. Mama's here."

Shane pops into the nursery, presumably looking for Luke. He returns a moment later. "Where's Luke?" he asks Sam.

"Downstairs in the dining room with Molly and Jamie. They're feeding him breakfast."

Cooper walks into our room and slaps his hand on Shane's shoulder. "Everything's under control, buddy," Cooper says. "We'll leave you two alone so Beth can get comfortable in bed and nurse that baby. Holler if you need anything."

Once everyone is gone, I lay a very fussy Ava in her bassinet while Shane helps me change into a clean nightgown.

Once I'm settled comfortably in bed, leaning against a couple of pillows against the headboard, Shane hands me the baby. "Will you be okay for a few minutes while I run down to the kitchen and get you something to eat? You'll need something in your stomach so you can take your meds."

"I'm starving, thank you. And a decaf coffee with caramel creamer?" I ask hopefully. "Please?"

He laughs as he bends down to kiss me. "Anything you want, sweetheart."

While he's gone, I nurse Ava and try to relax. Staring down at her, I can hardly believe she's real. Marveling at her, I trace the curve of her cheek with the tip of my finger. "You'll have your daddy wrapped around your finger in no time," I tell her. "But just wait until you try to date."

As she suckles vigorously, I stroke the soft brown peach fuzz on her head and trace her perfect little shell of an ear. I examine each little finger and each tiny fingernail. When she wraps her fingers around the tip of my index finger, I smile.

There's a quiet knock on my door.

"Come in," I say.

The door opens and Lia pops her head in. "Can I come in?"

"Sure." I nod to the spot beside me on the bed. "Come sit down."

Lia kicks off her shoes and sits on the bed beside me, leaning against the headboard. "How are you feeling?"

I smile. "Good."

She frowns as she looks me over. "Don't bullshit me, princess. You've looked better."

I forgot who I was talking to for a minute. "Honestly, I feel like crap. Everything hurts. But I don't want to complain."

Lia nods. "I figured as much. I heard what happened, about part of the placenta being in there still." She makes a face. "How is that even possible? Anyway, I'm glad you're back home." Lia reaches over and stroke's Ava's cheek. "When she's older, I could give her self-defense lessons, if you want. A girl can't be too careful."

"I would love that, Lia. Thank you."

There's another knock at the door.

"Come in," I say.

The door opens, and Hannah and Sophie come in.

"We just wanted to check on you," Hannah says. "I hope it's okay."

"Of course," I tell her. "Come on in."

Lia's older sisters join us on the bed. It's rare that I'm with all three McIntyre girls at one time. I see Lia and Sophie regularly, of course, but not Hannah. This is a rare treat.

I notice Sophie watching Ava closely. "It won't be too much longer before you'll be holding your own baby," I tell her.

"It's hard to believe," Sophie says as she lays her hand against her rounded abdomen.

"Dominic seems excited," Hannah says.

Sophie nods. "He is. He's looking forward to having a family of his own."

"What about you, Hannah?" I ask her. "Are you interested in marriage? Kids?"

She makes a face. "Hardly. I spend half my days traipsing around in the back-woods. It's not an ideal place to raise a family."

Lia elbows her sister. "Oh, I'm sure Killian could be persuaded."

Hannah punches her younger sister in the arm. "Quit it. What about you?" She stares down pointedly at the ring on Lia's finger. "You're already engaged."

"It's just a ring," Lia says dismissively as she studies the slender gold band on her finger.

She acts like it's not significant, but I know better. She loves Jonah.

When Ava loses interest in nursing, I prop her up against my shoulder and pat her back. It's not long before we hear a quiet little burp.

"Good job, Ava," Lia says.

I pat her a few times to see if there are any more air bubbles needing to come out.

"Can I hold her?" Sophie asks when it appears we're done with the burping.

"Of course." I hand Ava over. A few minutes later, Hannah insists on having a turn.

Using his shoulder, Shane pushes open the bedroom door and walks in carrying a tray with a plate of food and two cups of coffee. "All right, you three, out," he says brusquely to his sisters. "Let Beth eat her breakfast and rest."

"Fine, kick us out," Lia grumbles as she heads for the door. She pauses before she steps out and glances back at me. "Feel better soon."

I nod. "Thank you."

As Hannah hands me Ava, Shane closes our door, sets the tray on my nightstand, and hands me a cup of coffee. "Decaf," he says. "With caramel creamer."

"My hero," I say, smiling as I take a sip. While I drink my coffee, I check out the breakfast plate: a stack of buttered pancakes with maple syrup, sausage links, and a piece of toast slathered with butter and strawberry jam. I have to eat so I can take my meds and keep my milk production up.

Shane holds out the piece of toast for me to take a bite. "Eat. Luke is downstairs with Molly and Jamie, who are doing a phenomenal job of entertaining our son."

I'm missing my son, but I'm relieved that Ava is fed and content and in the process of falling asleep. While I finish my breakfast, Shane changes Ava's wet diaper and lays her down in the bassinet to sleep. I take my antibiotic, and Shane checks my temperature—it's normal, thank goodness.

Then he turns off the lights and climbs into bed with me. "Nap time."

I roll onto my side, and he spoons behind me. He brushes my hair back and plays with the strands—something he knows I love. When he plays with my hair, I get the most delicious tingles.

I feel his lips on my shoulder, warm and gentle, and then his arm slips around me and he holds me close.

"I'll stay with you a while, and then I'll go check on Luke."

Exhaustion sweeps through me, and I can't hold my eyes open any longer.

18

Molly Ferguson

Watching Jamie take care of Luke is bittersweet. Jamie loves kids, and I know he wants one of his own. I do, too, or at least I used to think I did when I was younger. But so much has happened since the idealistic days of my youth. I had a breast cancer diagnosis, surgery to remove both breasts, followed by my marriage slowly falling apart to the point that it turned abusive. I'm thirty-five now, no longer a spring chicken. And there's my cancer to think about. Even though I've had a double mastectomy, there's always a small chance it could come back. They can't remove *all* of the breast tissue—at least a tiny bit is left.

I don't spend my life dwelling on my bout with cancer or worrying about what the future might bring, but the facts are always there, deep in the recesses of my mind.

Would it be fair for me to marry Jamie?

What if my cancer comes back?

Jamie is the most selfless, most compassionate and loving person I've ever had the fortune to know. He has so many good qualities, and so much love to give. And he'd make a fantastic father. Even blind, he's capable of anything he sets his mind to.

Luke has finished eating his waffles and drinking his milk from a sippy cup. Jamie's doing a great job keeping him occupied while Shane and Beth are upstairs resting after their ordeal. Luke's been asking for his parents on and off all morning, but so far, we've managed to distract him. There haven't been any toddler tantrums yet.

We hear a bit of a commotion in the hallway, and then Jake and Aiden come bounding into the dining room, both dressed in swim trunks and practically vibrating with excitement.

Aiden is carrying a blow-up dinosaur swim toy. "We're going swimming!" he says, a huge grin on his adorable face. His brown eyes are big and bright, and he's clearly excited.

"I'm taking the little guy swimming while his sisters nap," Jake says. "You guys want to join us?"

Luke's eyes get big, too, when he sees Aiden's bright green dinosaur floaty. He starts jabbering and slapping his hands on his high chair tray.

"I think somebody wants to go swimming," I say to Jamie.

Luke climbs to his feet and throws himself toward Jamie, who catches him easily and pulls him onto his lap. "You wanna go swimming, buddy?"

Squealing, Luke bounces up and down on Jamie's thighs.

"I think that's a yes," I say, laughing.

"That's definitely a yes," Jake says.

"All right, buddy, hold on," Jamie says. Then to me, he asks, "Do you know if Beth brought any swim diapers?"

"I believe there are some in his diaper bag," I say. Since we're on babysitting duty, we have his diaper bag in our room.

"We'll be right down," Jamie says to his brother. "As soon as we get this guy cleaned up and changed."

Aiden literally jumps for joy, bouncing excitedly on his feet. "Luke, we're going swimming!"

Luke hauls himself up onto his feet and throws his arms around Jamie's neck.

"Okay, we're going, we're going," Jamie says and laughs.

When Jamie hugs Luke back, my heart melts. This man needs to be a father.

* * *

After washing off Luke's sticky fingers, we take him upstairs to our room to change him into a swim diaper.

"I'll do it," Jamie says as he lays Luke on our bed. "Can you hand me the diaper?"

I watch with great amusement as Luke squirms and rolls with excitement, reaches for his stuffed kitty toy, and tries to get up before Jamie's done. He's just being a typical toddler, and Jamie takes it all in stride with the patience of a saint.

"Hold still, little man," Jamie says with a laugh. He's using Cooper's nickname for Luke. "I only have two hands, you know."

It's fascinating to watch Jamie with the little ones. It's like he has a sixth sense about what they're going to do next. I've noticed he keeps one hand on them at all times—I think that's how he can anticipate their every action before they take it. I suspect he feels their muscles contracting before they actually make the move.

Luke squeals as he tries to roll away half naked, but Jamie stops his getaway attempt with one hand while he tugs the swim diaper in place.

Jamie's the first one to volunteer to change a diaper, wipe sticky little fingers, or wash a dirty face. I suspect he's trying to demonstrate his child caretaking abilities, but he doesn't need to prove anything to me. I know he's incredibly competent at everything he sets his mind to.

Once the swim diaper is in place, Jamie pulls Luke up to stand on his feet. "Ready to go swimming?"

Luke bounces on the bed, chattering like crazy, and then he launches himself into Jamie's arms.

Jamie smiles. "Let's get changed."

I take over babysitting duty while Jamie goes into our closet and changes. When he's done, I change into my navy blue one-piece swimsuit. When we're all ready, we head downstairs to the poolroom, where we find Jake and Aiden already in the water, playing in the shallow end as Aiden floats in his dinosaur.

Jamie sets Luke on his feet, and the toddler pulls him toward the pool.

"You guys go ahead," I say as I take a seat on one of the poolside loungers. "I think I'll just watch for a while."

I never tire of watching Jamie in the pool. As a former Navy SEAL, he's completely at home in the water. Even blind, he navigates the pool with an uncanny ability.

After putting some pint-sized armband floaties on Luke, Jamie carries him into the pool.

Jake splashes Aiden, which makes the little boy squeal with delight. It's wonderful how Jake has taken so readily to being a father. Not only is he the father of twin baby girls now, but he has also legally adopted Aiden, Annie's son from her first marriage.

I'm pretty sure Jamie envies his two brothers who have recently become fathers. And his sister Sophie will join the parenting ranks soon.

Jamie's sitting in the shallow water with Luke in his lap. Luke keeps lunging for Aiden's floating dinosaur. To distract him, Jamie carries Luke deeper into the pool, where the water is waist-high on Jamie. Jake pulls Aiden along, and the four of them are near the middle of the pool.

Luke suddenly seems a bit leery of the water, and he clings

to Jamie like a little monkey, his legs wrapped tightly around Jamie's waist, his little hands clutching Jamie's shoulders as if his life depends on it.

Jamie rubs Luke's back and says something to him, obviously trying to comfort him. He bobs in the water, just enough to get Luke's feet wet, and Luke chortles with glee as he begins to relax.

Jake says something to his brother, and Jamie nods. Then Jamie hands Luke over to his brother and pulls Aiden from his dinosaur floaty.

Holding Aiden, Jamie sinks down into the water so that only their heads are above water. Jamie says something to Aiden, who nods hesitantly. Then Jamie carefully rolls Aiden over onto his back and holds him as he teaches Aiden how to float on his back. At first, Aiden is tense, and he has a death grip on Jamie's hands. Jamie slowly walks him around in the water, showing him how to position his body so that he stays afloat. Jake watches with an approving smile.

After a few minutes of practice, Jamie releases Aiden's hands and coaches him to float on his own. After some misguided attempts, Aiden succeeds. Jamie steps back from the boy as Aiden floats on his own.

"Daddy, I'm doing it!" Aiden yells. "I'm floating."

Jake hands Luke back to Jamie and he scoops Aiden up into his arms. "That was awesome, buddy. Good job."

"I can swim now," Aiden says.

Jake laughs. "Well, let's not get too carried away."

I can hear the guys talking about swimming lessons. While they're deep in conversation, I wade into the water and take Luke from Jamie. Luke clings to me, his little legs around my waist and his tiny hands fisting the straps of my swimsuit. I walk around the pool, bobbing with him in my arms. Gradually, he relaxes enough to laugh when we bob up and down in the water.

Luke points toward the pool entrance and squeals with delight when he spots Shane walking in. "Dada! Dada!"

Shane comes to stand at the side of the pool, his hands on his hips.

I walk over to the edge with Luke and hand him up to Shane. "Looking for this little guy?"

Shane nods. "Beth wants him. I think she's having withdrawal." He grabs a dry towel from a cart and wraps it around his son before perching him on his hip. "Thanks, Molly. We appreciate you and Jamie watching him for us."

"Anytime," I tell him.

Jamie swims over toward us. "How's Beth?"

Shane readjusts his hold on Luke, who's tucking his head into Shane's chest. "She's doing about as well as can be expected. Her fever is down, but she's in some discomfort."

"Dada," Luke says, reaching up to pat Shane's bearded cheek.

Shane leans down and kisses the baby's head. "Hi, buddy. I missed you."

"And the baby?" I ask.

"Ava's doing well. Right now, Beth needs rest more than anything, but I think she's having trouble settling down without Luke." Shane lifts Luke high up, bringing their faces level with each other. "Ready to go see Mama?"

Luke's expression morphs into a big grin, and he kicks with excitement.

After Shane and Luke leave, Jamie asks me if I want to swim laps with him.

"Sure, but I'll just slow you down," I tell him. I'm a decent enough swimmer, but I don't have the strength to keep up with his powerful strokes.

He wraps his arms around me and pulls me close for a kiss. "I'll take it easy on you, I promise."

19

Jamie McIntyre

As we swim laps together, I'm careful to match Molly's pace so she doesn't fall behind. We swim shoulder to shoulder from the shallow end of the pool to the deep end, and back again. Besides Jake and Aiden, who are waging a splashing war in the shallow end, we have the pool to ourselves.

I really enjoyed taking care of Luke this morning. I love that little guy and love spending time with him. I enjoy spending time with all my nieces and nephews, but if I'm being honest, I have an ulterior motive. I want to demonstrate to Molly that, despite being blind, I'm perfectly capable of taking care of children. I'd be a good father and a good husband. I know I would be, because I'd give them everything I had—every bit of me. I'd never stop striving to be what they need.

Molly has never once made me feel that she thinks otherwise, but she wouldn't be human if the thought didn't occur to her. We've talked about marriage, and she knows I want us to have a family, but we haven't made any concrete plans. Something's holding her back, and I'd be stupid not to wonder if it's my blindness.

Is she willing to saddle herself with a blind partner? Is she willing to have children with one?

We swim laps for about twenty minutes—until I hear her struggling to catch her breath. I think she's had enough. She hasn't conditioned the way I have.

As we approach the shallow end of the pool, I stand and snag her hand and pull her close. "Ready for a break?"

"Yes, thank you," she says, panting as she tries to catch her breath.

After we dry off, we head back up to our suite to change clothes. Molly opts for a shower so she can wash her hair to get the chlorine out. I sit out on the balcony in the late morning sun and listen to the sound of the wind blowing through the trees and the rhythmic sound of lake water lapping against the shore. I hear a yacht's horn off in the distance, accompanied by the low growl of a pair of jet skis.

After my accident in the military, I recuperated here at this house. Kenilworth was my home for a long time, while I struggled with depression and PTSD. It became my safe place.

It's here that I learned to navigate my way through a home. This is where I learned to hone my remaining senses. Elly taught me to cook and do my own laundry. She taught me to be self-sufficient.

But after a while, I grew restless. Shane and Elly had made living here too comfortable for me. They saw to everything I needed, and it eventually made me feel less of myself. That's when I knew I had to move out on my own and test my abilities. I craved independence. So I moved into an apartment building in Wicker Park, and that's where I met my new neighbor—Molly.

I never had the pleasure of seeing Kenilworth myself. I was already blind when I arrived here. But Molly, with her artist's vision, described the landscape so vividly that I felt I could see it. In my mind's eye, I could picture this house and how it sits on the land. I could see the lake perfectly, the blueness of the sky, the white clouds. I could picture the collection of boats moored at Shane's private dock, the long grasses that grow on the slope heading down to the private beach. Thanks to Molly, I could see it all in my mind.

Back when I could see, I took it for granted, of course. Don't we all? But I don't live in the past. I don't mourn for what I lost. No, I live in the present—and presently, I am a blind man who loves a woman who, I suspect, is afraid of the future. Afraid of what might or might not happen.

The glass door behind me slides open and Molly steps out onto the balcony. She smells like vanilla-scented soap and mint toothpaste.

"It's lovely out," she says as she comes to stand behind me. She leans down and wraps her bare arms around me and rests her chin on my shoulder. "There's not a cloud in the sky, which is a bright cerulean blue. The tree limbs are swaying gently in the breeze, their bright green leaves contrasting brilliantly against the blue of the sky."

She's my eyes.

Smiling, I turn to face her, and we kiss.

"You were great in the pool with Luke," she says. "He had such a big grin on his face. He loves the water. Aiden does, too."

"They both need swimming lessons. It's a practical matter. All kids need to know how to swim."

She tucks my hair behind my ear, her touch sending a heated shiver down my spine. "And their Uncle Jamie is the perfect person to teach them."

I grab her hand and pull her around in front of me and sit her on my lap. After capturing her hand, I bring it to my lips to kiss. When my hands settle on her hips, I realize, to my pleasant surprise, she's naked. "You're naked," I say as I skim my hands up her torso, then back down to her ass.

She laughs. "I am."

Knowing her bare butt is on my lap, I can't help but respond. My cock hardens, pressing against my jeans. "If you're going to prance around me naked, then I think the least you can do is marry me."

I hear the swift intake of her breath.

This isn't the first time I've asked her. Or the second. But each time I've broached the subject, she has gently changed it.

She sighs. "Jamie."

I link our fingers together. "What are you afraid of?" I know she loves me, and she knows I love her. There's never been any doubt of that. But something is holding her back from making a commitment. I have to ask her the obvious question. "Is it my blindness?"

"God, no!" she cries, clearly offended that I'd even suggest it. She pulls her hand free and cups my face. "Jamie!"

I smile guiltily because I know it was a sneaky, low blow. She has no problem with my lack of sight. "Do you think I can't take care of you? Or that I can't take care of our future children? Because I can. I—"

She turns to straddle my lap. "You know better than that," she says, practically growling the words. Her hands cradle my face once more, and she leans in to kiss me, her mouth simultaneously sweet and hot. Strands of her wet hair fall against my cheeks, cool and smelling of peppermint.

"Then please, for God's sake, woman, show me some mercy. Say yes. Tell me you'll marry me."

She sighs as her lips graze mine. She kisses the tip of my nose, then my closed eyelids, then my forehead. "Jamie—" She hesitates to say more.

"Tell me what's holding you back. Just say it. If it's not my blindness, then what is it?"

She's silent for a long moment—so long I'm afraid she's not

going to answer me. Then, she says, "I'm thirty-five, Jamie. On top of that, I've had breast cancer. It's possible it could come back one day. And I know how much you want a family—children. I have no breasts. I can't—"

"Stop." I grasp her face in my hands and make her face me. Even though I can't look her in the eye, I know she can read my expression. "Last time I checked, having breasts isn't a prerequisite for having babies. And yes, it's possible your cancer could come back. It's also possible I could get hit by a bus tomorrow. Life doesn't come with guarantees, baby. We go for what we want and hope for the best. What I want is to be married to you, share my life with you. And if we're lucky, we'll have a family in the process. And if we don't, then we have each other. Tell me you don't want that, too."

"I do, but—"

"No buts." I reach into my jeans front pocket and pull out the gold band that I carry everywhere with me, just in case. "Let me put this ring on your finger, Molly. Right now. Please."

She laughs softly as she nuzzles my face. "How can I resist such a romantic gesture?"

"To hell with romance. I tried that and it didn't get me the answer I wanted. Now I'm going for direct. Marry me, Molly Ferguson. Take pity on a blind man and say yes."

She leans closer, and I feel her breath against my ear. Then she whispers, "Jamie McIntyre, there's absolutely nothing about you to pity."

"Then say yes."

She sighs. "Yes."

My heart slams into my ribs. "Yes? Really?"

"Really."

"So if I tell my family at dinner tonight that you've agreed to marry me, you won't contradict me?"

She laughs. "I won't. I promise."

"I'm holding you to it," I say. I set her off of me so I can stand. Then I sweep her into my arms and carry her back into our room. "This definitely calls for a celebration," I tell her as I somewhat gently toss her onto the bed.

She laughs again, and the sound wraps around my heart.

I follow her down onto the bed and roll onto her.

"Aren't you a bit overdressed?" she says as her hands skim over my chest and down to my hips.

I shiver when I feel her fingers unfasten my jeans. I don't need any other encouragement. I shuck off my clothing—all of it. When I come back to her, she pulls me close.

20

Beth McIntyre

I'm awake and sitting up on the side of the bed when Shane returns to our suite with Luke in his arms.

As soon as he sees me, Luke reaches for me, stretching out his little arms as far as he can. "Mama," he wails as he bursts into tears.

I hold out my arms, and he falls against me, his tear-stained face pressing against my chest. "Hello, sweetheart," I say, and then I kiss his forehead.

He climbs up onto me and presses his face to mine. "Mama."

"Be careful, buddy," Shane says, reaching for Luke. "Don't

hurt your mama."

"He's okay," I say. "I don't mind if he climbs on me." I've missed him terribly.

"At least let me change him first," Shane says, scooping Luke into his arms once more. "He's soaking wet."

That's when I realize Luke must have just come from the pool. He's wearing a wet swim diaper, and the chlorine-scented pool water is soaking into my nightgown.

Of course when Shane pulls Luke off me and carries him into the nursery, Luke starts crying in earnest. Fortunately, Ava sleeps right through the noise. I guess she'll have to get used to sleeping through lots of noise.

In record time, Shane returns with a dry toddler in a clean diaper and dressed. He deposits our son on the bed. Luke crawls to me and cuddles up against my body. I wrap my arms around him, smiling when he yawns.

Shane laughs. "Somebody needs a nap. Swimming is hard work." Shane climbs into bed with us, and we watch as Luke drifts off to sleep, his little thumb tucked securely into his mouth.

"I used to suck my thumb," I say as I watch my son sleep.

"Our little miracle," Shane says as he pats Luke's back.

"He is a little miracle," I agree, thinking back to his rocky start to life.

Shane strokes Luke's hair. "I can't wait to watch him grow into his role as big brother."

I smile. "If he's anything like you, he'll be a wonderful big brother."

Shane reaches over Luke and threads his fingers through my hair. He leans close and kisses me gently. He's a master at the art of kissing. "I love you, Elizabeth Marie Jamison-McIntyre."

I laugh. "That's a mouthful. Now kiss me again."

* * *

I must have dozed off again because a while later, I awake feeling so much better. My body doesn't ache quite as much, and I can move more freely without discomfort.

Shane's lying in bed, wide awake, Luke sitting astride his belly. While Luke plays with his stuffed kitty toy, Shane pretends he's trying to take it from him. Luke laughs uproariously.

"I'm sorry we woke you," Shane says, turning to look at me. "We were trying to be quiet."

Stretching, I yawn. "It's okay. I've been sleeping too much lately."

We hear a quiet rustling coming from the bassinet. I sit up and gaze down at Ava, who's starting to wake. But she's not quite there yet. Her eyes flutter open. A moment later, she lets out a tentative cry.

"Baby," Luke says, pointing at the bassinet.

"Can you say *Ava?*" Shane asks him.

"Baby."

Shane laughs. "Maybe one day." Then he asks me, "Ready for

some lunch? I'll run down and get us something and bring it back here. We can eat in bed."

"Eat," Luke says, looking very interested in the idea.

"That sounds wonderful," I say. "I'm not quite ready to get dressed and face the world yet."

Not long after Shane leaves us to get our food, I hear a quiet knock on our door. "Come in."

The door swings open and my brother, Tyler, and Ian poke their heads inside. "Can we come in?" Tyler asks.

"Sure."

Ian sits on the bed while Tyler stands, checking me over.

"How are you feeling?" Ian asks as Luke crawls to him and pulls himself up to stand.

"Much better."

"Fever gone?" Tyler asks.

"Yes. I think I'm on the mend."

Tyler looks around. "Where's Shane?"

"Getting us some lunch."

Ava starts making urgent little squeaks.

"Can I get her?" Ian asks, eagerly glancing toward the bassinet.

"Sure."

Ian stands and hands Luke to Tyler. Then he walks to the bassinet and peers down into it, a smile on his handsome face. "Aren't you the sweetest little cutie pie I've ever seen?"

I smile as Ian reaches into the bassinet and carefully lifts Ava into his arms. He cradles her gently to his chest and walks back toward Tyler, holding the baby for my brother to see. "Have you ever seen anything more adorable?"

Shane walks into the bedroom carrying a tray of food and drinks. "Lunch is served."

21

Jonah Locke

After lunch, I grab Lia's hand and pull her out the front door. "Let's go see the horses."

"Okay," she says, eyeing me suspiciously as we step outside.

We pass Haley and Philip, who are seated on the front steps, deep in conversation.

"Hey, guys," Lia says to them. "Don't do anything I wouldn't do."

"Is there anything you wouldn't do, Lia?" Philip asks with a laugh.

"Don't be a smart ass, Phil," Lia says. "I kicked your ass once before. I can do it again."

Haley's eyes widen. "You did?" she calls after us. "Seriously, Lia?"

"Yep," Lia yells back. "Knocked him out cold. Just ask him. He'll tell you all about it."

We walk across the circular drive and down the well-worn path that leads to the barn. Lia's blonde hair is pulled back into a single braid, and she's dressed in cargo pants and a black T-shirt that says "Nope" in white letters.

I really hope that T-shirt isn't prophetic.

She leads the way into the barn, where it's cool and dark. The air smells earthy and sweet, a combination of fresh-cut hay, molasses, and manure.

When she climbs up onto a stack of hay bales and sits, she's at the perfect height for me to pull her close and wrap my arms around her hips.

She threads her fingers in my hair, which is currently up in a topknot. When she scrapes her nails over my scalp, I can't help groaning.

"You like that?" she says just before she leans down to kiss me.

"You know I do." I pull her closer and step between her thighs. When I look up at her and lock onto her crystal blue gaze, my chest heats. She mesmerizes me—she has ever since we first met. I thought the effect would gradually wear off, but it hasn't. If anything, it's grown more intense.

"Did you bring me out here to make out?"

I can't help grinning. "Not exactly, although it is a good idea." I bring her hand to my lips and kiss the back of it.

"Then why did you bring me out here? I know you're up to something."

I gaze down at the engagement ring on her finger. "I have an idea."

"And what's that?"

"Marry me."

"Jonah." She sighs in exasperation because I've asked her to marry me a thousand times, and she's said *yes* a thousand times. The problem is, she won't commit to a date.

I know Lia. She hates the idea of getting dressed up and standing in front of a room full of people. She hates the idea of being the center of attention, of having all those eyes on her. I thought if we decided to just do it—spontaneously—that she'd consider it.

I reach into my front pocket and pull out a slim gold wedding ring, which I hold up to her. "Marry me right here and now. This afternoon."

Her eyes narrow with a mixture of confusion and skepticism. "What the hell are you talking about?"

"Let's get married this afternoon, right here at your brother's house. Your family is already here. We have a captive audience. And you don't have to do a thing but stand there and say *I do*."

She rolls her eyes. "Get real. We can't just do that."

"Yes, we can. Cooper still has a valid license to perform weddings. We can walk in there right now, just as we are, and Cooper can say the words. Quick, simple, easy, done. We'll be married before dinner."

Her eyes narrow on me. "You're serious."

My heart pounds as I meet her gaze. "I'm dead serious, Lia."

She narrows her eyes. "I don't have to wear a dress or put on make-up or do anything fussy with my hair?"

I try hard to suppress my grin. "Right. You don't have to do a thing. Come just as you are."

Her eyes narrow shrewdly. "If I agree to do this, then you'll finally stop asking."

It's not a question; it's a conclusion. I nod. "That's right."

"Okay, fine. Anything to shut you up about it." She slides off the hay bales, grabs my hand, and pulls me toward the door. "Let's get this over with."

As we walk back to the house, I grab my phone from my back pocket and shoot Cooper a text.

Jonah: She said yes! We're doing it.

Cooper: It's about damn time.

And then I chase after Lia, who's moving like the hounds of hell are after her.

Lia beats me to the front door, but I catch up to her in the foyer. I grab her hand and pull her around to face me. "You do want this, right?" I ask, just to be sure. I know her snarky attitude is just a front, but I have to be sure. Yes, I'm pressuring her, but only because it's the only way this is ever going to actually happen. I'd never force her to do something she doesn't want to do. "I love you, Lia, and I want to spend the rest of my life with you. Please tell me you feel the same."

She rolls her eyes at me. "Do you really think you could pressure me into doing something I don't want to do?"

"Well, no."

"Of course not." She grabs my shirt and pulls me to her. "I don't do anything I don't want to do." And then she kisses me hard and fast. "Now let's get this over with before I get cold feet."

Smiling, I grab Lia's hand and pull her to the great room, where most of her family is congregated. Most importantly, her parents are here. Bridget's sitting with Annie and Sophie on a sofa, holding the twins. Calum is hanging out with the guys around the bar. They're not drinking—it's too early for that. But the bar is the de facto boys' hangout.

"Listen up," Lia says, drawing everyone's attention.

I bring her hand to my mouth to kiss it, then release it so I can cross the room to Calum. When I reach him, I stand before him, look him in the eye, and say, "Mr. McIntyre, I'd like to request permission to marry your daughter."

Calum's gaze shoots over to his daughter. Bridget jumps to her feet, her expression a mixture of shock and excitement.

As Calum studies his youngest daughter for a very long moment, my pulse kicks into overdrive.

"Lia, is this what you want?" he asks her.

She nods.

Calum nods, looking almost relieved. "All right then." He offers me his hand, and we shake. "Welcome to the family, son."

The room explodes into action. Bridget and Sophie descend on Lia, hugging her.

From behind the bar, Cooper checks his watch. "It's one-thirty. When are we doing this?"

"Right now," I say, hoping to keep this train on track.

"We need time to get ready," Bridget says, her gaze jumping from Lia to Sophie to Annie.

"We're doing this now, Mom," Lia says. "There's nothing to get ready. That's the whole point."

Bridget lays her hands on Lia's shoulders and pulls her closer. "Honey, this is your big day. You can't just get married without doing a few things."

Lia's gaze narrows as she tenses. "Like what?" she asks. "And if you mention a dress, I'm leaving."

Sophie laughs. "Well, how about a bouquet, at least? Surely we can come up with some flowers quickly."

Lia shakes her head. "There's no time. We're doing this now, or not at all."

My stomach sinks. I know the ladies are trying to be helpful, but if they're not careful, they're going to ruin the whole thing. The more time Lia has to fret over things, the likelier she is to call the whole thing off.

"Will you guys excuse us a minute?" Bridget says as she pulls Lia out the door into the foyer. Sophie and the other girls follow them.

Oh, man. Please don't screw this up for me.

22

Lia McIntyre

"Mom—"

"You need something borrowed and something blue," my mom says as she stands there wringing her hands. "It's tradition."

I'm sure this isn't how my mom pictured one of her daughters getting married. I survey the small crowd forming around me—Mom, Sophie, Hannah, Annie, Sophie, and Elly. "All right, fine. Does anyone have anything blue?"

"I do," Annie says, holding up her right hand and pointing at a ring on her finger—a ring with blue stone surrounded by tiny

diamonds. "It's a sapphire ring Jake gave me for my birthday."
Annie takes off the ring and hands it to me. I slip it on. It's a little too big for me, but it will do. "How about anything borrowed?"

"How about this?" Sophie asks as she unclasps a gold chain bracelet from her wrist and offers to put it on me. "It belonged to Dominic's mother. He gave it to me after we were married."

"Great, thanks," I say as she attaches it around my wrist. "Now we're good, right?" I glance around at the group, at all their uncertain expressions. *Jesus, this could go on forever.* "This is it, right? We're done?"

"But what about the flowers, honey?" Mom says, wincing apologetically. "We have to have flowers. The bride needs a bouquet, and your bridesmaids. And who will be the flower girl? Haley could do it. She's the youngest female here. And Aiden could be the ring bearer."

"Mom." Hannah lays her hand on Mom's shoulder. "Lia doesn't need all that to get married. We're keeping it simple, remember?"

I sigh heavily. Thank God for Hannah. Of all my siblings, I think she gets me the best.

"Maybe just one bouquet?" my mom asks, sounding hopeful.

"Wait," Elly says as she snaps her fingers. "I have an idea. Just give me five minutes." And then she heads for the kitchen.

"What's going on?" Erin says as she walks down the staircase with Haley.

"My baby's getting married," Mom says.

Erin's eyes widen. "Really?"

I roll my eyes. "Yes, really. Although the longer this takes, the more I'm rethinking the whole idea."

"Congratulations, Lia," Haley says. "That's fantastic."

"I don't know. I'm honestly starting to have my doubts."

The front door flies open and Elly races in holding several long-stemmed giant purple flowers. "How about these?" she asks, breathless. "They're Summer Hydrangeas from my garden."

"Oh, Elly, they're perfect!" Mom says. "Do you have a ribbon or some twine?"

Elly nods. "I have some twine in the kitchen. I'll be right back." Then she races off again.

"Flowers, check," I say. "That's it. I have everything I need. Will someone please tell Jonah we need to get this show on the road?"

"What about Beth? And Molly?" Sophie says. "They're not here. And I think Shane and Jamie are missing too."

"I'll go get them," Hannah says as she heads for the stairs.

Needing a moment alone, I cross the foyer to stand in front of a window that overlooks the front drive. This is escalating so quickly, and I don't know how to slow it down without bailing on Jonah completely. And I don't want to do that to him. He deserves better from me.

I'm not stupid. Jonah's the best thing that's ever happened to me. I'm a pain in the ass, and I don't know why he puts up with me. He could easily be with some cute, perky girl who wants all the things that normal people want. Instead, he's with me—a snarky, sarcastic, anti-social, smart-mouthed, nonconforming pain in the ass.

I stare fixedly at the fountain in the center of the circular drive and watch the water cascading down into the pool below, hoping to drive everything else out of my head.

A moment later, I feel hands settling comfortably on my shoulders. I don't even need to look. My entire body responds, and I lean back against a familiar, firm chest.

Jonah rests his chin on my head. "Doing okay?" he asks quietly.

I don't hear any other voices. I think everyone's vacated the foyer, probably to give me space. "Did someone fetch you?"

"Yeah. Sophie did."

I nod. "It's mushrooming out of control."

"I know. I promised you no fanfare. I said we'd just stand up in front of Cooper and say *I do*. I'm sorry it's escalated."

I turn to face him and slip my arms around his waist. "Can we just do this now, please?"

"Yes. Right now." He cups my face and leans down to kiss me. "I love you, Lia."

"You could have chosen a lot better for yourself."

Jonah laughs. "No. I think I lucked out. I've never been so happy and felt more content than I do with you in my life."

Elly sidles up next to us and hands me the bouquet of giant purple flowers tied up with a twine bow. "All set," she says.

Jonah offers me his arm, and I link my elbow with his. We

walk across the foyer and into the great room.

A hush falls over the room.

Everyone is here, seated around the room or standing at the bar, staring at us in anticipation. Even Beth managed to come down from her room. She's seated on one of the sofas next to her mom, who's holding Ava. Annie and Bridget are seated with them, each holding a twin. Shane and Jake are standing behind the sofa, Shane holding Luke, and Aiden is perched high up on Jake's shoulders. I scan the room quickly—Philip, Liam, Miguel, Tyler, Ian, Killian, Sam, Mack. Everyone.

Cooper, dressed in black slacks, a white dress shirt, and a black tie, is standing in front of the glass doors that lead out onto the patio. He's the only one who actually dressed up for the occasion.

Wait.

Cooper dressed up for this?

That means he had to have known ahead of time.

"You planned this," I say to Jonah.

He grins at me. "You bet I did. I figured something impromptu was my best bet."

As we walk toward Cooper, I shake my head. "You're an idiot. Of all the girls you could have—of all the girls who literally throw themselves at your feet on a daily basis—you want to commit to *me*?"

When we reach our destination, Jonah turns me to face him. He cups my face in his hands and gazes down into my eyes, which are suspiciously threatening waterworks. "There's only one woman I want, Lia, and that's you."

I search his gaze, looking for something. "Why me?"

Jonah's smile fades. "I wish you could see yourself the way I see you. Why you? Because you're fierce. Because you're strong. Because you're sexy as hell. I can't imagine a better partner in life. Every time you walk into the room, my pulse races. My breath catches in my chest, and I feel like I'm the luckiest man alive. It's *you*, Lia. Only you. I can't picture a future without you in it."

My eyes tear up, and I blink the moisture away. My throat is so tight it hurts to speak. "I don't deserve you."

"It's not about deserving, Lia. It's about finding your other half. You *are* my other half. Please let me be yours."

I snort with laughter. "Oh, please, don't be so melodramatic. It's no surprise you're a songwriter."

Amidst the quiet chuckles in the room, Cooper says to me, "Lia McIntyre, do you take Jonah Locke to be your lawfully-wedded husband?"

I glance to my side at all our friends and family who are silently watching.

Jonah squeezes my hands. "Look at me, not them," he says.

I turn back to face Jonah. "I do," I say past the lump in my throat.

Cooper addresses Jonah. "Jonah Locke, do you take Lia McIntyre to be your lawfully-wedded wife?"

"I do," he says in a strong voice.

"Do you have the rings?" Cooper asks.

Jonah digs into his pants pocket and pulls out the slim gold band he showed me in the barn.

My stomach sinks. "I don't have a ring," I hiss at him.

"It's okay," Jonah says as he slips the ring on my finger. "I didn't think about that."

"Wait!" My dad steps forward and twists his own wedding band off his finger and hands it to me. "Use this."

My dad's wedding ring weighs heavily on my palm. "Let's hope this fits," I mutter as I slip it onto Jonah's ring finger. It's a bit big for him, but it'll do the job. "We'll go ring shopping when we get home."

As Jonah nods, I hear a few muffled sniffles coming from the audience.

"Now you may kiss the bride," Cooper says. "That is, if she'll let you."

The tension in the room is broken by laughter.

With a relieved sigh, Jonah pulls me into his arms and says, "You're stuck with me now, wife."

Wife.

Holy shit. What have I done now?

Now it's my turn to laugh. "Hey, don't blame me if you wake up one day and wonder why the hell you're stuck with me."

"Not a chance, tiger," he says, and then he dips me in his arms and kisses me in front of everyone.

The next thing I know, Mom and Dad are beside me, pulling me away from Jonah. My mom wraps me in her arms until Dad pulls me away from her and gives me a big bear hug.

Then my sisters are there, and I hug them both. Sophie has tears in her eyes. Then my brothers line up, from oldest to youngest, and I hug each of them in turn.

Jonah stands aside and watches with a contented expression on his face. His smile says, *We did it.* His smile is infectious. Yes, we did it. We're over the hump. The hard part is done. Yes, there's still the legal piece of this we need to complete. But this was the challenging part, at least for me—standing up in front of a room full of people—even the people I love most in the world. The rest is just paperwork—that's a piece of cake, and we'll get to that once we get back home. Right now, for all intents and purposes, we're husband and wife.

I smile when Shane claps Jonah on the back and pulls him in for a hug. "Well done, Jonah. I thought she'd never do it."

Jake joins us, one of his baby girls in his arms. I still can't tell them apart, but I'm not the only one, so I don't feel too terribly bad about it.

He grins. "So, if today is your wedding day, does that make tonight your honeymoon?"

I roll my eyes at him and hold out my hands to the baby in his arms. "Evvy?" I ask, nodding to the baby.

Jake shakes his head. "Emmy. But nice try."

"Gee, thanks." I laugh. "I had a fifty-fifty chance of getting it right."

Jake's right, though. Technically, tonight is our honeymoon, and the thought makes me feel suddenly a bit anxious.

I'm going to have sex tonight with my *husband.*
Holy crap.

23

Lia McIntyre

I'm married. I honestly didn't see this coming. The bastard blindsided me. But the good news is that he'll shut up now about us getting married.

I stare at my new husband with fresh eyes. He's mine now. *We're married.* He really is too gorgeous for his own good. His long, dark hair is up in a topknot, and his big dark eyes are glittering with happiness. I've honestly never seen him so happy.

I think of all the fans whose hearts will break when news of our marriage gets out on social media. "Just think of all those broken hearts," I tell him.

Elly brings out a beautiful three-layer cake, decorated with white icing, pale red roses, and fresh sliced strawberries, my favorite. Jonah must have given Elly a heads-up prior to us coming for her to have a wedding cake ready.

My twin comes up behind me and lifts me off the ground. "Congratulations, sis." He kisses the back of my head. "I'm happy for you."

I punch him hard in the arm. "Put me down."

Jonah drags me over to the cake and hands me a long, serrated knife. "You cut first."

Jesus, I'm a married woman. The realization hits me like a ton of bricks, nearly knocking the breath out of me.

Do I feel any different? No.

Well, maybe I feel a bit relieved that it's over and done with. And I must admit, it's kinda nice knowing this guy is stuck with me for the rest of his life.

I cut a piece of cake and hold it up to Jonah to take a bite.

Then he cuts a piece for me, and as he holds it to my mouth, there's a devious gleam in his eyes.

"Jonah, if you shove that cake into my face, you'll be sleeping in the barn tonight with the horses. Is that clear?"

He hesitates a moment before nodding. "Crystal clear. I wouldn't dare risk my honeymoon night."

Honeymoon? I roll my eyes. Good lord, don't remind me.

After we've had our bite of wedding cake, Elly steps in and cuts slices for the rest of the family.

Aiden's first to get a piece. "You're a married lady now, Aunt

Lia," he says, smiling up at me. "Congratulations."

I reach down to ruffle his hair. "Thanks, kid."

I help out by passing the empty plates to Elly. She sets a piece of cake on each one and gives them to Jonah, who hands them out.

Everyone's wishing us well, patting Jonah on the back and hugging me. My parents come up last to get some cake, both of them teary-eyed.

Mom pulls me into her arms and holds me tight. She's practically shaking. "I'm so happy for you, my sweet girl," she whispers into my hair. "All I want is for my kids to be happy." She kisses my cheek and pulls back. "Are you happy?"

I blow out a shaky breath and nod. I glance over at Jonah, who's looking at me like I'm the center of the universe, then back to my mom. "Yeah. I am."

Then my dad wraps me in another bear hug, nearly squeezing the breath out of me. "Four down, Bridget," he says to my mom with a wink at me. "Just three more to go."

"Don't hold your breath, Dad," Hannah says as she comes up behind us and puts her arm across Dad's shoulders. "I'm not getting married anytime soon."

After we eat cake, Cooper and Jake man the bar, along with my dad. Most of the guys hang out there, talking and laughing. The women hang out on the sofas and chairs, along with the little kids. Haley, Philip, Hannah, Liam, and the rest of the cool crowd hang out on the back patio.

Jonah and I join the guys at the bar.

Shane pulls me close as he makes a toast. "To Jonah and my baby sister. Here's wishing you both a long and happy married life." After everyone takes a sip of their respective drinks, Shane says, specifically to Jonah, "Good luck, pal."

It's a festive atmosphere as the sun starts to set. It's our last night here at Kenilworth. Tomorrow, everyone will head back to Chicago and our normal routines. Hannah flies black to Colorado early in the morning. I won't see her again until Christmas.

Jonah pulls me aside, then into his arms. He kisses the top of my head. "So, how does it feel to be a married woman?"

I wrap my arms around his waist. "It doesn't suck."

He laughs. "Any chance I can talk you into a dance? You know, our first dance as a married couple?"

"Never gonna happen."

His grin widens. "I didn't think so."

Sophie walks up behind me and taps me on the shoulder. "Hey, sis?"

"Yeah?"

"The girls and I were talking—we're wondering if you'd like to go out tonight. Sort of a bachelorette party. We could go out for drinks in town. Just us girls."

Lia's eyes widen. "I'd freaking love it."

24

Sophie Zaretti

"I never thought I'd say this, but we're having Lia's bachelorette party." I shake my head in disbelief as we head out to the front drive—Lia, Hannah, Erin, Haley, Annie, and Molly. Unfortunately, Beth won't be able to join us as she's recuperating, but she sent us out with her best wishes and told us to have a fantastic time.

"Will wonders never cease?" Hannah asks, rolling her eyes.

"Don't get your panties in a twist," Lia snaps back. "It's just an excuse to drink."

"Remember, Haley's only seventeen," Annie gently reminds

us. "Not too much drinking, right?"

Since there are so many of us, we decide to take Annie's minivan, which seats eight.

Before we walk out of the house, Mack pulls me aside, along with Lia and Hannah. "Keep an eye on Haley—she's underage. That means absolutely no alcohol. I'm serious. And watch out for Erin. She gets anxious in crowded public places, especially when they are a lot of strangers around—namely men."

I pat Mack's rock-hard bicep. No one has forgotten the horrific assault Erin experienced not that long ago. "We understand, big guy. Please don't worry."

Jake pulls Annie into his arms and kisses her. "Have fun, honey. Don't do anything I wouldn't do."

"Ha, funny," Annie says as she kisses him back. "That's not saying much."

Dominic stands behind me, with his arms wrapped around my torso as he gently rubs my baby bump, his chin resting on my shoulder. "Have fun, babe." He presses his lips to my ear and whispers, "But not too much fun."

Mack puts his arms around Erin. "Maybe one of us should go with you ladies."

Of course, by *us*, he means one of the men. "No," I say. "It's a *bachelorette* party, Mack. That means girls only. If you want to have a bachelor party, you guys can do that here while we're gone. Besides, Lia will be with us—she's a freaking professional bodyguard. And frankly, Hannah is just as skilled as Lia when it comes to hand-to-hand combat. So relax."

Mack is blatantly scowling. There's no other word for it. He's *so* not on board with this idea.

"Seriously, dude, chillax," Lia says as she claps him on the back before stepping down onto the drive. "I'll look out for all my chickies."

After we climb into Annie's minivan and buckle our seat belts, I glance out the front windshield at the collection of grumpy guys standing on the front steps. Namely Mack, Jake, and my Dominic. Jake and Dominic look bummed, as if they feel left out because their women are going out without them. Mack, on the other hand, looks truly worried, and honestly, he has a right to be. I know that Erin's emotional health has really suffered after her assault.

I glance back at Erin, who's sitting in the middle row of seats. "Are you okay, sweetie?"

Erin tucks her straight black hair behind her ear and smiles, showing perfect dimples in her round cheeks. But her blue eyes are shadowed with anxiety and misgiving. "I'm fine," she insists. "Really."

"Erin, you don't have to go—"

"I want to," she says adamantly. "I do." And then she betrays herself by glancing out the window at Mack, who's standing rigid on the front steps, his arms crossed over his chest. "This is a good step for me," she admits. "I need to go out more on my own—I mean without Mack. I rely on him as my security blanket way too much."

"All right. But if you feel uncomfortable for any reason, you tell us and we'll come straight home. Got it?"

She nods. "Got it."

Annie's driving, since we're taking her minivan. I'm in the front passenger seat as I'm pregnant and don't feel like climbing into the back. Molly and Erin are in the middle row, and Lia, Hannah, and Haley are in the back row of seats.

We take off for town, passing through both security checkpoints on the property. Old man Charlie is manning the intercoms, and he lets us through. It's a quick five-minute drive to the little downtown heart of Kenilworth, which is a quaint little shopping area made up of a few restaurants, a bar, a laundry mat, two gas stations, an ice cream shop, a grocery store, and a handful of other assorted businesses.

"Where to, ladies?" Annie says as she pulls into an off-street parking lot.

No matter where we decide to go, we're within easy walking distance.

Lia points down the street. "How about that place? The All-Star Bar and Grill? It's a sports bar, family friendly." She nods toward Haley. "You know, kids are allowed."

Laughing, Haley bumps shoulders with Lia. "I'm not a kid."

"That sounds like a good place as any," Molly says. "We can get appetizers and drinks... well, those of us who can drink." She nods toward Sophie. "Obviously, you and Haley can't."

"I can't drink either," Lia says. "I'm too young and impressionable."

Hannah elbows her sister hard. "Give me a break."

The seven of us cross the street and walk two blocks to the restaurant. It's dark out now, but the streetlamps are on, illuminating the sidewalks.

Hannah opens the door, and we all file into a small waiting area. The hostess gets a name and checks her seating chart. "Give us a few minutes to clean off a table for you guys. It won't be long."

While we wait in the bar area, a bar tender takes our drink order. Most everyone orders beer. Haley and I order Cokes.

"Nothing for me, thanks," Erin says.

Annie and I make eye contact. That's right—Erin was drugged in a bar. Her attacker snuck the date rape drug into her drink, and when she was partially incapacitated, he forced her up to his hotel room. No wonder she's so nervous and wary of accepting anything to drink.

"Do you want me to see if we can get you a sealed bottle?" I ask Erin. "Water or juice? Or a soft drink?"

Erin shakes her head. She's hypervigilant now, her gaze sweeping the area around us as if she's expecting a monster to jump out of the shadows. "Nothing, thanks. I'm just not thirsty."

Of course that's most likely a lie. She's probably scared to death.

We're in a sports bar, so it's not surprising there's a Chicago White Sox game playing on all the TV screens—well over a dozen of them. Fans are cheering the replay of an earlier game— one the Sox won, of course.

Thank goodness we arrived when we did because a charter bus pulls up to the restaurant and an entire team of college baseball players streams into the restaurant.

We're seated not long after. We decide to order just about every appetizer on the menu and share—hot wings, nachos, fried onion rings, potato skins, soft pretzel bites, and fried dill pickles.

Our server brings us a fresh round of drinks, and our appetizers arrive soon after.

I raise my glass—this time a virgin strawberry daquiri—and makes a toast. "To my baby sister. Congratulations, Lia, on *finally* tying the knot with one of the hottest guys on the planet. I hope you have some great sex tonight to commemorate the occasion."

As everyone laughs, Lia says with a straight face, "We always have great sex."

"Just wait until the news gets out on social media," Haley says. "His fans are going to freak out that he's off the market."

Just our luck—the traveling baseball team is seated across the aisle from us, taking up a number of tables They're loud, obnoxious, and drinking way too much booze. My guess is they were already well on their way to being trashed before they even got here. From the noise they're making, it sounds like they're celebrating a big win tonight.

I hear a couple of cat-calls and whistles that I suspect are being directed at our table. I do my best to ignore them and hope the others do too.

"Hey, ladies. Looking for a good time tonight?"

"Hey, sugar. How about we hook up? Our hotel is just down the street."

We're just about done with our appetizers when our server returns to our table carrying a tray of seven shot glasses containing clear liquid.

Frowning apologetically, the young woman holding the tray says, "These are for you guys—vodka shots, courtesy of the guys over there." She tilts her head toward the tables across the aisle from ours.

"No, thank you," Annie says, glaring at the players. "Take them away. We're not interested."

After our server leaves, two of the guys approach our table, both in their early twenties. They're still dressed in their team uniforms, with dirt-stained knees. One has short dark brown hair, and the other is blond.

"Hey, ladies," the blond says. "We're staying at a hotel just down the street tonight. Wanna join us for a little after-game party? Help us celebrate?" While he speaks, his gaze roams hungrily over the younger women—Haley, Lia, Erin, and Hannah.

Erin's staring down at her folded hands in her lap. Haley's looking anywhere but at the guys. It's Lia and Hannah I'm most concerned about; they both look like they want to shred these guys.

The dark-haired guy winks at me, then at Annie and Molly. "You sexy MILFs are invited, too."

Lia sets her beer glass down hard on the wooden table and levels an icy glare on the two players. "I'm sorry, but what gave you pathetic losers the impression that we'd be interested in a bunch of prepubescent dick wads like you?"

Haley snorts out a laugh and then quickly covers her mouth.

Momentarily stunned, the two guys look at each other, then back at Lia. Then they laugh.

"Oooh, I call dibs on the blonde bitch," the blond guy says. Then he has the audacity to run his hand down the front of his uniform slacks, stroking himself.

Lia motions to herself. "You want some of this, pal?" she says, egging him on. "You think you can handle it?"

The two guys laugh, as do their eavesdropping friends back at their table.

I glance at Erin, who's sitting frozen in her seat between Haley and Lia. Her expression is stone-faced, and her complexion has turned sickly pale. I catch Molly's and Annie's gazes. We need to leave now, I mouth to them.

Molly nods as she pulls out her wallet, withdraws some cash, and lays it on the table. Annie and I do the same.

"Let's go, guys," I say as I slide out of the booth.

"Time to go," Molly says to the other girls as she rises to her feet.

Lia and Hannah head straight for the exit, with Erin and Haley right behind them. The rest of us follow behind to make sure these assholes don't speak to Erin again. Haley's annoyed, but she doesn't look concerned. It's Erin we're worried about.

Once we step out onto the sidewalk, I take a deep breath, sucking in the cool evening air. "That was unpleasant," I say.

"Asshats," Lia grumbles as we start down the sidewalk toward the parking lot.

We don't get a hundred yards away before we hear renewed catcalling and whistles following us. Lia and Hannah pivot instantly and step around us, putting themselves between us and the idiots.

"Go to the vehicle," Hannah says as she and Lia stand side-by-side on the sidewalk, watching the guys approach. There are five of them, and from the way they're carrying themselves, I'd say they're all drunk.

"No, Lia." I put my hand on her shoulder. "We're all going. Together."

Lia shrugs me off. "Go, Soph. We'll join you in a minute.'"

There's no way we're leaving Lia and Hannah here to deal with these assholes alone. Annie pulls Erin behind her, and Molly does the same with Haley.

"Come on, guys," I say. "Let's just go."

But it's too late for that. The guys run up on us, sweaty and disheveled from their game, no doubt.

"Why'd you run off like that?" the blond guy asks. "We were just trying to be friendly." He stumbles and falls into his dark-haired friend, and they both almost tumble to the ground.

Yep, they're drunk.

Lia steps forward, getting in the blond's guy's face. "Why don't you and your moron friends get lost?"

The blond's expression morphs instantly into a belligerent sneer. "Why don't you shut your bitch of a mouth? Or at least put it to good use." And then he grabs his cock and makes an obscene gesture.

"Calm down, Cody," his dark-haired friend says as he grabs the guy's arm and attempts to pull him back.

The one named Cody pulls out of his buddy's grasp.

The rest of the guys are starting to fan out around us, caging us in. *Shit.* This isn't going to end well. Someone's going to get hurt. Namely them.

"Come on, fellas," I say, hoping to defuse the situation. "Go back to the restaurant and leave us alone."

"Shut up, bitch!" Cody growls. But his gaze is locked on Lia.

I glance back at Erin, whose arms are wrapped tightly around her torso. Her blue eyes are huge in her pale face, and she's literally shaking. Haley notices, too, and puts an arm around Erin.

It's time for an executive decision because we need to get Erin out of here. "All right, do it, Lia," I tell her. Then I take out my phone and take some pics of these assholes in case we need photographic evidence.

Then I nod to Annie and Molly. "We have to go."

Five of us resume our walk to the van, knowing that Lia and Hannah won't let the idiots follow us. We don't get more than a dozen feet away before we hear the scuffle, followed by grunts and cries of pain.

I look back to see Lia standing over Cody's prone body. He's not moving, so I assume he's out cold.

"That's what you get for being disrespectful to women," Lia grounds out as she digs her boot into the guy's belly. He still doesn't move. "Wimp."

Hannah has his buddy in a choke hold, his arm twisted sharply behind his back. He's grimacing in pain as he sinks to his knees.

The three other morons stand there indecisively as they weigh whether or not to get involved. When Lia takes a step toward them, they scatter and run back to the restaurant, leaving Cody and his friend on the sidewalk.

As Lia wipes her hands on her cargo pants, I smile at my little sisters. They are both kick-ass bitches. "Well done, ladies," I tell them. "Let's go."

When we arrive back at the house, the guys are outside waiting for us—all of them. I called ahead to let Dominic know what happened, so he could give Mack a heads up. Now they're all waiting outside for us—Mack, Dominic, Jake, Philip, Jamie, Jonah, and Killian. And they're pissed.

"Oh, wow," Annie says as she parks the minivan and peers out the passenger window. "Look at that wall of angry male testosterone."

As Molly smiles, I fan myself. "You have to admit, that's hot."

Mack is at the vehicle even before Annie has shut off the engine. He opens the door and helps Erin out.

Dominic opens my door and peers inside the van. "You girls all right?"

"We're mostly fine," I say, taking Dominic's hand as he helps me out of the vehicle. I glance at Mack, who has his arms wrapped around Erin. "Erin's not fine."

Jake and Killian are standing beside the van, both of them looking grim. Jake looks Annie over as she steps out onto the drive. "Are you okay, babe?" he asks his wife. I can tell he's holding back rage.

As Hannah exits the van, Killian's gaze skims her from head to toe, but wisely he doesn't say a word.

Lastly, Lia and Haley hop out.

Jonah steps forward and eyes Lia. "I heard you kicked some ass."

Lia nods. "He was scrawny, though, so it wasn't much of a contest."

Mack holds his hand out to Haley. "Are you okay?"

"I'm fine, Dad," Haley says, not seeming a bit upset. "You should have seen Lia and Hannah! They were awesome. They sent those perverts running for their lives."

"All right, everyone inside," Annie says. "We've had enough excitement for one evening."

25

Mack Donovan

I'm so fucking livid I could break something. I *want* to break something—like the necks of the assholes who scared Erin.

Dominic frowns as he relays the news to me. "Sophie assured me no one touched a single hair on Erin's head, and Lia took care of the bastard."

But that's not good enough. That asshole scared the shit out of her.

Haley, on the other hand, seems fine. Actually, she seems pretty excited about the whole thing. I leave her downstairs with the others, who are retelling the story to a captivated audience, and take Erin upstairs to our room.

As soon as we step inside the privacy of our suite and I shut the door, Erin wraps her arms around me and holds on for dear life. She's shaking like a leaf.

"I'm so sorry, honey," I tell her as I hold her close. My words are lame, but I don't know what else to say. It's a fucking shame she couldn't go out with her friends to a restaurant without being accosted by idiots. And I don't want to fly off in a rant and stress her out even more.

I lead her over to an oversized upholstered chair, sit down, and pull her onto my lap. I turn her sideways and pull her legs up, tucking her feet beside my leg.

"It was awful," she says. "I was afraid to drink anything. Sophie offered to get me a sealed bottle of something, but I couldn't even do that. And then those guys started saying things to us and catcalling. They wanted us to party with them in their hotel room."

I still. "Seriously? They asked you girls to hook up with them?"

"Yes. So we left. Some of them followed us out of the restaurant as we were walking back to the van. That's when Lia and Hannah took on two of them. The rest ran back to the restaurant. Lia knocked one of them unconscious."

I'm enraged but trying hard not to let Erin see it. She doesn't need any more stress. But something needs to be done. I'm not going to let this slide.

There's a knock on our door.

"Come on in," I say.

The door opens, and Jake, Annie, Sophie, and Dominic walk in. They all seem pretty subdued, but I can tell Jake and Dominic are as mad as I am.

"Hey, guys," I say.

Jake steps forward, his expression tight. His jaw is clenched hard, and I know he's keeping his cool because of Erin. He looks me in the eye. "Annie and Sophie will stay with Erin."

I nod.

Hell, yes. Of course we're going after those motherfuckers.

Erin turns her gaze on me. "What are they talking about? Are you going somewhere?"

"Yeah, honey," I tell her. I brush her bangs aside. "I won't be gone long, and you won't be alone. They'll stay with you until I get back."

Erin's eyes widen and she looks frantic. "No! You can't leave. Where are you going?"

I hate to add to her anxiety, but there's no way in hell we're letting this stand. "Erin." I brush my thumb across her soft cheek. "We're not letting those guys get away with this."

"You're going after them?"

I nod. "The three of us are, yes. Annie and Sophie will stay with you until I get back."

She studies me a moment, then looks to the others. Jake and Dominic are two hulking walls of muscle, and there's absolutely nothing that could stop them from exacting revenge on these thugs.

The only thing that could keep me from leaving right now is Erin.

"Please, honey," I say. "I need to do this."

As tears well up in her blue eyes, she nods. "Just don't be gone long, okay?"

I cup her face with my hands. "I won't. I promise."

I give her a gentle kiss, then rise to my feet and seat her in the chair. "I'll be right back."

It kills me to leave Erin right now, but I know she's in good hands. She won't be alone. Right now, this is something I need to do.

When the three of us get down to the foyer, we're met by a small army—Killian, Liam, Philip, Sam, and Miguel.

"Thanks, but we got this, guys," Jake says to them.

"We're coming, too," Liam says. "All of us."

"They harassed people we love, our friends," Sam says. "We're not letting that slide."

"Fine, suit yourselves," Dominic says as he heads for the front door. "Let's go."

We split up into two vehicles as we head for the hotel where we think the baseball team is staying. Sophie sent us the pics she took before the altercation took place on the sidewalk, so we have clear images of the two assholes who were the real problem.

When we arrive at the hotel, we see a charter bus in the parking lot with baseball graffiti sprayed on the windows. We're definitely in the right place.

Before we even vacate our vehicles, a rowdy crowd of young guys comes walking through the parking lot. They're still wearing their uniforms, stained with dirt.

We exit our vehicles and surround them before they know we're even here.

"What the hell?" says a blond guy who's got a swollen right eye that's already turning shades of black and blue.

This must be the one Lia knocked out.

"What happened to your eye?" I ask him.

"None of your fucking business," the blond says. By the way he's slurring his words, it's clear he's drunk off his ass. He's also not quite steady on his feet.

"He got punched by a girl!" yells one of the other guys, and they all start laughing uproariously.

"Shut up!" the blond kid yells. "It's not funny."

I stalk over to the blond until I'm right in his face. I grab him by his uniform collar and lift him high enough off the ground so that we're eye to eye. "She should have done a hell of a lot more than punch you, asshole."

"Jesus, Cody, do you know this guy?" yells one of the other players.

Cody starts struggling as he tries to pry my hands off his shirt. "Let me go, you motherfucker!"

I set him down on the ground, hard. He nearly stumbles to the ground. I get right up in his grill, my teeth gritted as I say, "You don't go around disrespecting women, moron. Not unless you want to deal with their irate boyfriends." Then I haul back my arm and make a fist, intending to give him a second shiner.

But before I can hit him, I detect the strong odor of hot urine. I glance down and notice that the guy has wet his pants. "Jesus, you're a fucking coward."

Some of his friends notice the wet spot on his uniform pants and resume laughing.

"Hey, man," one of the players says as he nervously scans the men surrounding them. "It was Cody and Doug who were hitting on those girls. The rest of us didn't do a thing. We're sorry, man. It won't happen again."

I release Cody suddenly, and he falls on his ass, hitting the pavement hard. His pants are soaked through, and his teammates renew their laughter.

"It's not funny!" Cody yells, choking back tears.

"No, it's not funny," I agree. "It's pathetic. *You're* pathetic."

* * *

As soon as we return to Kenilworth, I high tail it upstairs to the room I share with Erin. Annie and Sophie are still with her, of course. When I walk into the room, they turn to look at me expectantly.

"It wasn't much of a fight," Jake says as he walks into the room after me, followed by Dominic.

"Pretty much a big let-down," Dominic says. "The blond coward pissed himself, literally. It was embarrassing."

Annie rises to her feet and walks into her husband's arms. Jake hugs her tightly and kisses her forehead.

"Mission accomplished?" she asks him.

He nods. "As well as can be expected. They were kids. Our options were limited."

Annie nods. "I understand. Still, I'm sure you made your point."

The two couples leave our room, and I shut the door.

"It's late," I say to Erin. "You ready for bed?"

She nods. "I just want this day to be over."

"I understand. While you're getting ready for bed, I'll run down and check on Haley and say goodnight to her. I'll be back before you miss me."

Erin gives me a smile—the first one I've seen since they returned from the ill-fated bachelorette party. "Impossible. I'll be missing you the moment you walk out that door."

26

Bridget McIntyre

I still can't believe my baby girl is married. Well, nearly married. I know they still have to take care of the paperwork, but that's just a formality. The important thing is that Lia said *I do* in front of a room full of people. She stood up with Jonah, in front of Cooper and all of us, and pledged herself to Jonah.

I'm still pinching myself.

"You must be thrilled, Bridget," Ingrid says.

"I'm over the moon." Laughing, I wipe at my teary eyes. "I was so afraid Lia would never go through with it—she just can't stand being the center of attention. Poor Jonah has been so patient and tried so hard to get her to settle on a date. He was smart to do it spontaneously."

"He *knows* her, Bridget," Ingrid says. "Probably better than anyone. Kudos to him."

Calum walks into the great room. "Well, that's all done. The guys are back."

"Did they find those awful young men?" I ask.

Calum nods. "Put the fear of god in them, from what I heard."

"Poor Erin," Ingrid says.

Calum takes my hand and pulls me close. "Ready for bed?"

"I am. Lead the way."

"I have to hand it to Jonah," Calum says as we climb the stairs. "He knows our daughter well. Sometimes I think he knows her better than she knows herself."

As we walk up the stairs arm in arm, he says, "Four kids down; three more to go."

When we reach our room, I pull a nightgown out of a dresser drawer. When I turn, Calum's undressing. I pause a moment to admire the view. At sixty-five years of age, he's still a very handsome and fit man. His trim gray hair only adds to his appeal, making him look quite distinguished.

He catches me eyeing him. "You like what you see?"

I grin. "You know I do. Where do you think all our handsome sons got their good looks?"

Calum laughs as he walks toward me in nothing but his boxers. I take in his broad chest and firm biceps. His years as a firefighter honed his body, and he hasn't gone soft since he retired. Of course, he works hard around the house, taking care of the property and his collection of classic cars, helping out the kids, chasing after our grandson Aiden—it keeps him in shape.

He cups my face in his big hands. "And where do you think our beautiful daughters got their looks from?" He leans down to kiss me. "Watching Lia standing up there tonight—she reminded me so much of you on our wedding day. Of all our daughters, she takes after you the most—the same sweet face and freckles, the same blue eyes. It just about choked me up."

Calum threads his fingers through my hair, which is hanging loose and curly today, just at my shoulders. I'm sixty, and I have more than my fair share of silver strands already—I attribute them to being the mother of seven strong-willed children. But they blend into the strawberry-blonde strands so well that they're pretty well camouflaged.

My husband glances down my torso. "Someone still has her clothes on."

My cheeks heat as I smile. Sliding my hands down the sides of Calum's torso, I come to the waistband of his boxers. "Someone still has his boxers on." I go up on my toes and kiss him. "Give me a minute to get ready for bed."

I disappear into our bathroom to freshen up for bed. He follows me in and does the same. As we stand side by side at the bathroom counter and brush our teeth at the his-and-her sinks, our gazes meet in the mirror.

We've been married for nearly thirty-eight years now, and

we're the parents of seven grown children and one baby angel in heaven. The day I met Calum McIntyre was the luckiest day of my life—it was also the day he saved my life. But the real blessing was falling in love with him and receiving his love in return.

Finished in the bathroom, we walk out together, and Calum turns off the light behind us. He slips up behind me and wraps his arms around my waist. His lips graze the side of my neck, sending shivers through me.

"You still have too many clothes on, woman," he says as he reaches around to unbutton my blouse.

We may have been married for nearly four decades, but the fire still burns hot between us. Every day I wake up next to this man, I count my lucky stars.

Calum's hands slip around me, right beneath my breasts, and he kisses the side of my neck. "This weekend was a nice break for everyone. It's good to have all the kids under one roof. The grandbabies, too."

I can't believe we have five grandchildren now, soon to be six when Sophie and Dominic's baby arrives. And I have a pretty strong feeling that more grandbabies will be forthcoming. I wouldn't be surprised if Jake and Annie have more children, and Shane and Beth, too. What I'm really hoping is that Jamie and Molly will tie the knot and start a family. I know how much my second son wants to be a father and husband.

Then we just have to wait on the younger three to catch up and start families of their own.

Calum pulls my blouse off me and tosses it onto a chair. Then he unfastens my skirt and skims it down to my ankles. He unfastens my bra, dropping it, and slips my panties off me. I'm standing bare naked in front of him while he's still in his boxers.

When I shiver from head to toe, he grins as he reaches around me to cup my heavy breasts. Then he starts working kisses down my neck and across my shoulder. One of his hands slides down my torso, past my waist, until he cups me between my legs. When he presses up against me, I feel the ridge of his erection nudging me from behind.

My breath catches in anticipation, and I moan softly as my head falls back against his shoulder. My legs are like jelly now, threatening to give out on me. When his fingers slip between my legs and start teasing me, my belly quivers.

Without warning, he scoops me up into his strong arms and carries me to the bed, laying me down gently. He's a big man, strong and powerful, but he treats me like I'm made of spun glass.

His gaze locks onto mine as he strips quickly. "You take my breath away, Bridget McIntyre." He climbs onto the mattress, crouches over me on all fours, and leans down to kiss me. Pretty soon he's working his way down my body, pausing to kiss my breasts, flick my nipples gently with his tongue, then down to my belly button and farther below.

I gasp when I feel his tongue between my legs. My fingers latch onto his hair, and I show him want I want.

Soon I'm panting for air and my cries are loud.

Dear Lord, I hope no one can hear us.

27

Lia McIntyre

After the guys get back from their vengeance raiding party, Jonah and I say good night to everyone and head upstairs to our room. As realization hits, my stomach starts doing somersaults.

This is my honeymoon night.

Granted, we aren't going away for our honeymoon, but it's our first night together as a married couple. Is that going to change anything? I doubt it. But still, it's a momentous occasion.

Once we're in our room, with the door closed and locked behind us—just in case any exuberant well-wishers decide to pop in to congratulate us—Jonah surprises me by leading me out onto the balcony.

I laugh. "What, you're not just going to rip my clothes off and have your way with me?"

"Not quite yet, no. We need to talk."

Uh-oh. Those are the four most hated words in the English language. "Talk about what?"

When we're outside, facing the lake view, Jonah takes my hand in both of his and holds it to his chest, right over his heart. We stand, facing each other, and the tension is so thick I could cut it with a knife.

"Just spit it out, Jonah," I blurt out.

He winces. "I just need to be sure, Lia. Really sure."

"What are you talking about?"

"Our wedding was so spontaneous and impromptu. I just want to make sure you didn't feel pressured into doing something—"

"All right, rock star, stop right there. Since when am I the type of person who gets pressured into doing anything she doesn't want to?"

He smiles. "Well, normally you're not. But today was different. We got *married*, Lia. And to be honest, that's something you've been resisting for quite a while. I need to be sure you're happy about that, and that you didn't feel pressured into it. Remember, it's not even legal until we sign the papers. If you change your mind or want to back out, you can at any time. I won't hold it against you, I promise."

"Would you please shut up and kiss me?" I grab his shoulders and pull him down so our mouths are level. "Since this is our *honeymoon*, I think there should be less talking and way more kissing."

He's smiling, but he's still not done. "I'm serious. If you're not one hundred percent sure—"

"For god's sake." I take his hand and pull him back into the bedroom. First things first, I grab the hem of his sweatshirt and lift it up. He helps me by whipping it over his head and dropping it to the floor. I whip off my T-shirt and toss it aside, too, quickly following with my bra.

He just stands there, his gaze locked on my breasts.

"You are such a boob man," I say as I reach for the fastener on his jeans. I tug them down his legs, along with his boxer-briefs. His erection springs free.

"You're enjoying this, aren't you?" I ask. "The idea of married sex."

Reaching for me, he grins. "I am."

I pull back out of his reach. "How about a honeymoon blow job from your *wife*?" I wrap my fingers around his length, tighten my grip, and gaze up into his eyes.

Jonah's gaze darkens as he stares down at me, his expression hungry.

Oh, yeah, he wants this.

I back up, pulling him with me, until I hit the mattress. Then I sit and spread my legs, drawing him to stand between them. When I lean forward and run my nose along the length of him, breathing in his heated scent, he groans and fists my hair.

"Jesus, Lia."

I chuckle. "Oh, we're just getting started, buster."

Since this is his honeymoon blow job, I'm going to make sure it's a damn good one.

As I lick the length of him, from his balls to the crown, he arches his back and growls his pleasure. I circle the head of him with my tongue, tasting salty pre-cum, and his fingers dig into my scalp.

After I've teased the hell of out of him, I draw him into my mouth and take him deep. He groans loudly, which thrills me, and his breaths come in rapid pants. I struggle with insecurity, but when I hear him make raw, guttural sounds like that, it mollifies me. Maybe I *am* enough.

I love blowing Jonah. I love watching his arousal grow. I love feeling his strength and his power and knowing it's for me. Taking him deep into my throat, I stroke him with my tongue, teasing and licking and jacking his pleasure higher and higher. All the way to the back of my throat, I envelop him in tight wet heat, until he starts thrusting mindlessly, his breaths harsh and quick, his hands gripping my head. He tries to be a gentleman about it, but eventually he loses control and starts fucking my mouth.

His cock throbs wildly against my lips and tongue, and I know he's close to coming.

Suddenly, he pulls out and grabs hold of my hands. "Not yet," he says as he tries to catch his breath. He pushes me onto my back and pulls off my cargo pants and underwear and tosses them aside. Then he yanks off my shoes and socks, and kicks off his own. Now we're both naked.

Then he's on his knees beside the bed, shoving my legs open and draping them over his broad shoulders.

One thing I've learned about Jonah is that he's an equitable lover. He gives as good as he gets.

I lean my head back on the mattress and sigh because I know mind-blowing pleasure is coming. A moment later, I feel his breath between my legs, cooling my wet heat. Then his tongue flicks my clit, over and over until my nerves are singing. My belly starts quivering, and my thigh muscles tighten in anticipation.

My man knows how to go down on a woman. He knows how to make my body shiver and quake and sing. His finger slides deep inside my opening, and he strokes me until I'm squirming. As pleasure ratchets higher and higher, I squeeze my eyes shut tight and block out everything but him and the wonderfully wicked things he can do with this tongue.

A random thought enters my head.

My husband is going down on me.

Jonah is my freaking husband.

And that sends me right over the top. I bite my lip hard enough to taste blood as I try to keep from crying out. Pleasure races through my body, tensing every muscle, making me see stars as my orgasm sweeps through me. My entire body is alive and throbbing, shaking violently, and all I can do is feel pleasure.

He climbs up onto the mattress and kneels between my legs. My muscles are limp, and he arranges me the way he wants me, with my knees bent and my legs spread open wide, so that he can lean over me, his cock sinking deep into my wetness. He braces his palms on the mattress, one of each side of my head, and begins to move. It's fast and furious and perfect. He plows into me, hard, relentlessly, and we're both struggling to suck in air.

Jonah kisses me, his mouth hot and hungry. He steals my breath and gives me his. My fingers slide into his hair, and I grip his head tightly, holding him to me.

He's so hot and thick inside me, throbbing, and I feel the moment he climaxes, filling me with his heat. And he keeps thrusting as he revels in the feel of our bodies joined.

As he gradually comes down from the high, his kisses turn more gentle. He murmurs sweet nothings in my ear and strokes my hair and face softly. It's like he loses control, and then he feels like he has to apologize.

I pull him down on top of me, loving the weight of his big body on mine. We roll to our sides, still joined together, one of my legs splayed over his hip.

He kisses me. "Wife." There's so much satisfaction in his voice, in that one word.

I brush his hair out of his face. "Don't let it go to your head."

He laughs. "I wouldn't dare."

He runs his blunt nails down the center of my back, along my spine, and I shiver. Then he starts tracing patterns—first a heart, then the words *I, love,* and *you*. When he's done, his hand snakes up to grip the back of my neck and he kisses me for a very long time, until we're both breathless.

After we make the mandatory trip to the bathroom to clean up, we crawl back into bed and wrap ourselves in each other's arms. I'm wiped, and it's late.

"Go to sleep," he says when I yawn.

I skim my fingers down his chest. "You realize millions of girls are going to be heartsick when they find out you're married."

"I suppose so."

I reach for my phone.

He eyes me warily. "What are you doing?"

I grab his hand—the one with my dad's wedding band on it—and link our fingers together. I snap a pic of our hands that shows both of our rings, post it to Instagram, and add a caption that says, *Sorry, girls. He's off the market.* "Boom!"

Jonah laughs. "Oh, my god. Here comes the backlash."

"Too bad. You're taken."

"I was taken the day I laid eyes on you, tiger. We just finally made it official."

* * *

Early the next morning, my phone buzzes with an incoming message. Sleepily, I reach for it and check the screen and the time. It's just past seven.

"Who is it?" Jonah asks as he stretches.

"Hannah."

"Is she okay?"

I read her message.

Hannah: I'm leaving in an hour. Liam's driving me to the airport. Just wanted to say goodbye before I left.

Immediately, I hit the call button, and she answers on the first ring. I put the call on speaker.

"Crap," she says. "I hope I didn't wake you. I didn't realize it was so early."

"You didn't. We're up," I lie.

Then she laughs. "I'll bet Jonah's been *up* all night. Shit. It's your honeymoon. I shouldn't have texted you."

"It's okay. Jonah's still recovering. At his age, he needs a few minutes. By the way, you're on speaker."

Hannah groans. "Oh, double shit. Sorry, Jonah."

Jonah laughs. "No problem, Hannah. Have a safe trip back."

"What's up, sis?" I ask her.

"I just wanted to say goodbye in person, if that's possible. But I don't want to interrupt your honeymoon. I won't see you again until Christmas."

"You'll be back then?"

"Yeah."

Something's wrong. I can hear it in her voice. I put my phone on mute for just a moment, long enough to tell Jonah, "She sounds like she's been crying." I unmute my phone. "Hannah, is everything okay?"

"Yeah, sure."

"Honestly, you don't sound fine."

She sniffs. "It's nothing. I shouldn't have called. I'm sorry. I'll let you get back to it."

Then I hear a series of dull thuds that sound suspiciously like a gloved fist hitting a punching bag. "Are you in the fitness room?"

"Yeah. I woke up early and couldn't go back to sleep. I thought a workout might help."

"Want some company?"

She hesitates. "No, that's all right. You're busy."

"I'm not too busy for you." I sit up in bed and glance down at Jonah. He waves toward the door, motioning for me to go. "I'm coming down, Hannah. Be right there." And then I end the call.

"What's she upset about?" Jonah asks as he runs his warm fingers down my bare back.

"I'm not sure, but I have my suspicions." I climb out of bed. "Sorry to bail on you, pal, but sisters before misters."

Stretching, he chuckles. "Go."

I hop out of bed and take a super quick shower before I pull on a pair of clean underwear, my workout shorts, a sports bra, socks and sneakers. After brushing my teeth, I quickly braid my wet hair. Then I'm out the door and heading down to the lower level.

It's not unusual for Hannah to be up early. She's always been an early riser. When we were kids and shared a bedroom, she'd be the last one to bed and the first one to wake. Sometimes I wondered if she slept at all.

The fitness room is dark, with just one light on in the locker room. I flip on a set of overhead lights and dim them.

Hannah's standing in front of a punching bag, gloves on. She's covered in sweat, which means she's been going at it for quite a while.

I grab a pair of gloves and slip them on, using my teeth to secure the Velcro wrist straps. "You wanna tell me what's wrong?"

"No." She moves to the center of the mat. "You wanna let me kick your ass?"

I laugh. "No."

Hannah and I are pretty evenly matched when it comes to martial arts, but she's bigger than I am. She's a half-foot taller than me and a good twenty pounds heavier.

"So, Liam's taking you to the airport?" I ask as we circle each other on the mat.

She lunges forward, trying to fake me out. "Yeah."

"Not Killian?"

Her expression tenses. "No. Why should he?"

"He picked you up from the airport."

"Only because Shane asked him to."

I snicker. "*Sure*. Only because Shane asked him to."

Hannah throws a kick at my jaw, but I lunge back, out of range. Then I turn the tables on her, driving her back with a series of uppercuts followed by a right hook. When I succeed in catching her shoulder, she spins out of reach.

Hannah ducks beneath another kick. "I don't want to talk about him."

"Who? Shane?" Of course I know who she really means.

"No, idiot. Killian."

"Are you seriously not into him?" I ask her, giving her an incredulous look. "The man's fucking hot."

We're circling each other, both of us looking for an easy shot.

"Can we talk about something else?" she asks. "Like the fact that you got married yesterday. That was sneaky as hell, Lia. I didn't have time to get you a wedding present."

"I don't want one." I manage to drive her back with a couple of punches, followed by a kick.

"Are you happy about it?" she asks.

"About what? Getting married?"

"Yeah." She pushes me back, almost to the edge of the mat, getting several good hits in.

"Sure. I love Jonah," I say, breathing heavily now. "Honestly, being married isn't going to change anything. I don't care if we're married or not, but it matters to him, so I'm happy to oblige."

"You're lucky. He's a good guy."

"So is Killian. What's the deal with you two? Obviously, he's crazy about you, and you keep blowing him off."

Hannah stops in her tracks, her chest heaving as she tries to catch her breath. "I'm not like the rest of you. I'd never be happy back in Chicago, so it's pointless."

"You're making a lot of assumptions. Maybe Killian would relocate to Colorado to be with you."

Hannah laughs. "Sure."

"Have you ever asked him?"

Hannah comes after me with a vengeance, driving me back with a series of hits and kicks. "I'm not about to ask him to completely change his life, give up his job, uproot himself, and leave his friends. Just for me? Forget it."

"You'll never know if you don't give him a chance."

28

Killian Devereaux

Hannah's flying back to Colorado later this morning, and I heard she asked her brother Liam to drive her to the airport. Her brother, not me. I offered to take her. She said she'd *let me know*.

I feel this deep connection with Hannah. It's something I can't explain—it just is. When I look at her, it's like the earth stands still, and I find myself utterly captivated by her. I think it's her strength and resolve that I find so damn attractive. The woman can hold her own under any circumstance, and I find that a real turn-on. Where I come from, strong women are appreciated.

But unfortunately, the connection doesn't go both ways, because she won't give me a damn inch. It's confusing as hell because I catch her watching me sometimes. Her gaze follows me across the room. I know she's not oblivious to my existence, but for some reason, she keeps me at arm's length.

Restless, I put on a pair of shorts and head down to the lower level to the fitness room. A workout might help me center myself. At the very least, it'll help me burn off some of this pent-up energy.

It's just past seven, and the house is still dark and quiet. I imagine everyone's still sleeping. But as I approach the fitness center, I see a faint light shining through the viewing window. I suppose someone could be in there... or maybe someone left the light on last night. I walk up to the window to check, and to my surprise, I see Hannah sparring with her younger sister.

Lia and Hannah are a lot alike—both strong-willed and pig-headed. Both independent as hell. Jonah seems to have done a decent job reeling Lia in, but I've done nothing but crash and burn when it comes to getting Hannah's attention.

I stand in the shadows and observe the two girls going at it. I suppose I shouldn't be acting like a stalker, but the temptation of seeing Hannah in action—seeing what she's physically capable of—is too much to resist.

I already know that Lia's a beast in the ring. Whether it's kickboxing, Aikido, or Krav Maga, she's an outright terror. I've seen her knock guys twice her size on their asses. Lia may be petite, but she packs a powerful kick. It doesn't take long for me to realize that the girls are pretty evenly matched. They're going at each other pretty seriously, despite the sporadic laughter. Clearly, they're having fun.

I'm sure Lia misses her big sister a lot. Hannah only comes back to Chicago a few times a year for short visits. They don't get a lot of time together time.

They're both wearing gloves, boy shorts, and sports bras. Both have braided hair, Lia's blonde and Hannah's brown. I watch Hannah try to fake a punch, followed by a kick, but Lia dodges the blow and pivots away. I guess I shouldn't be surprised that Hannah knows what she's doing in the ring—after all Liam is her brother, too. And Liam's an international champ.

"What are you doing up?" Jonah Locke asks me as he comes to stand beside me.

"I could ask you the same thing. Isn't this your honeymoon?"

He laughs. "Don't worry. There was plenty of honeymooning going on last night. But Lia got a text message this morning from Hannah and decided to come down here and check on her sister."

Keeping out of sight, we watch the two girls go at it. I wince when Lia manages to get in a solid kick. "Damn."

"Yeah, they train hard. It takes some getting used to. But it's a good thing Hannah knows how to take care of herself. I hear the town she lives in is a bit rough—a real wild, wild west."

I nod. It's reassuring that Hannah can take care of herself. Still, I'll worry about her. From what I hear, she spends most of her time out in the wilderness, tracking everything from bears to wolves to mountain lions. After finishing her university degree, she now works for a nonprofit wildlife preservation organization. Their mission is to stop illegal trapping and poaching. *Damn.* That could turn sketchy real fast. And Hannah's out there in the forefront, chasing poachers who are probably armed.

She's bad-ass, and that's probably why I'm so damned attracted to her. She's a spitfire. A wildcat. And right now, watching her spar on the mat, my pulse pounds, and I can't take my eyes off her.

"Congratulations on your marriage," I tell Jonah, trying to distract myself from watching Hannah.

He nods, fighting a grin. "Thanks." Then he yawns. "I'm heading back to bed. I just came down here to make sure everything was okay. Looks like it is."

As Jonah heads back upstairs, I stay a little while longer. This is probably the last time I'll see Hannah for a long time.

Maybe forever.

The thought sinks in my gut like a stone.

29

Haley Donovan

Monday morning, after showering and dressing, I pack up my things and carry my duffle bag down to the front door, where a small mountain of luggage is piling up.

I head for the dining room, where I hear a ton of voices.

The room's packed, with well over a dozen people seated around the big table, along with three high chairs. Beth's mom is holding baby Ava while Beth feeds Luke something that looks like oatmeal.

It's kind of hard for me to identify with such a large family, as I'm an only child. My mom never had any more kids after she married my step-dad, and my dad has stayed single. He's with Erin now, and she's much younger than he is. I sort of suspect they'll get married one day and start having babies, which would be awesome. I still have a chance of becoming a big sister.

My dad asked me once how I'd feel if he and Erin got married and had babies. I told him, *Hell yeah. Go for it.* I even offered to babysit for free.

Erin saved a chair for me at the far side of the table. When she waves me over, I stop to grab a plate from the buffet line and fill it with bacon and waffles, lots of butter, syrup, and whipped cream. I even grab a few gigantic strawberries that are dipped in chocolate. One thing I love about coming here is the food—Elly spoils us rotten.

When I take my seat, Erin reaches over to hug me. "Did you sleep well?" she asks.

"Yeah." That's not exactly true, as I stayed up half the night because my mind was racing about Philip. Going home this morning means I probably won't see him for a while. It's hit or miss whether I run into him in my dad's apartment building.

Every time I see Philip, my feelings for him solidify even more. But Dad treats me like I'm a kid who doesn't know what she wants in life, and he treats Philip like an ogre who's hitting on someone too young for him. I'm seventeen years old, for god's sake. I'm not a kid. I'm old enough to know what I want.

I love my dad, but he's so overprotective. I think it's kind of ironic considering how young Erin is.

My dad reaches past Erin and squeezes my shoulder. "Good morning, honey," he says. "We'll be heading home after breakfast. Are you all packed?"

I nod. "My bags are by the front door."

Movement at the door catches my attention. I glance over to see the guy squad coming in for breakfast—Philip, Liam, and Miguel. They're all freshly showered after a morning run. I saw them leave the house together earlier this morning, from my bedroom window, which overlooks the front drive.

Right behind them are Tyler and Ian. I think that's everyone now, packed into this dining room. Everyone's talking at once, and it's hard to hear a thing. I'm not used to this much noise.

I stand and pick up my plate. "I'm going to take this outside," I tell Erin. I have to lean close enough that she can hear me.

She nods.

And then I make my escape.

It's much quieter in the foyer, but I slip out the front door and sit on the steps, propping my plate on my knees and eating in silence.

As I bite into a juicy strawberry, I hear the door behind me open. A moment later, Philip sits beside me on the top step.

"You okay?" he asks.

I nod. "I'm just not used to being around so many people at once. It's a little overwhelming."

He laughs. "I'm an only kid, too. I can relate."

I notice he doesn't have any food. "Want some of mine?" I ask him.

"No, thanks. I'm fine."

I doubt that's true. It must take a lot of calories to fuel that big body of his. All those muscles, long legs, and muscular arms require a lot of energy.

"Are you happy to be going home?" he asks me.

I take another bite of a strawberry, chew, and swallow. "Not really. It means I have to go back to school tomorrow."

School. That reminds me that I asked him to take me to the homecoming dance, and he said no. Rejection sucks. I never should have asked him in the first place—I'm such an idiot.

"At least it's your last year of high school," he points out.

My last year of high school. A lot of good that will do me.

Philip glances back at the door behind us, then to me. "I'd take you to your school dance if I could," he says, clearly reading my mind. "I'd love nothing more than to be your date. But we have to wait, Haley. You understand that, right? I'll be counting the days until your eighteenth birthday. It's not so far away."

As I turn to meet his gaze, I realize I could lose myself in those eyes. He's looking at me so intently, like he's trying to tell me something.

"Will that make a difference?" I ask.

He nods. "It'll make a huge difference. Once you're eighteen..." He lets the words hang there in the air between us.

Our eyes are locked on each other, like magnets. He reaches out as if he's going to touch my face, but he drops his hand. He's so damn chivalrous. I don't think my dad even appreciates how honorable Philip is.

"I've never known anyone like you," he says as he stares off into the distance, across the drive, toward the woods. "Some things are worth waiting for, Haley, you know?"

Mesmerized by his words, all I can do is nod. My pulse is racing now as I consider the possibilities.

"Look," he says. "I know it's not fair of me to ask, but if you'll wait for me—"

"I'll wait."

"I don't want you to miss out on your school dances. If there's someone you want to go with, it's cool."

"There's not. If I go, it will be with my girlfriends. Honestly, I don't even want to go if you can't go with me."

"I don't want you to miss out on your high school milestones, Haley. Those only happen once."

I shrug. "It's not important."

Before either one of us can say another word, Aiden comes running out the front door, followed by Jake, who is carrying multiple overnight bags.

"Hi, Haley. Hi, Philip," the kid says. "I'm helping my dad get the van because it's time to go home."

Aiden's practically bouncing on his feet as he clutches a worn dinosaur to his chest. I don't think I've ever seen the kid not excited about something.

Jake lays a hand on Aiden's head. "Wait here, buddy. I'll get the van."

"Okay!" Aiden squeezes himself down between me and Philip, completely oblivious to the momentous conversation he just interrupted. But I can't be mad at him. He's too young to realize.

"I had waffles, too," Aiden says as he surveys the uneaten food on my plate. "And strawberries." Then he glances up at Philip. "What did you have?"

"Nothing yet," Philip says.

"You can have some of Haley's," Aiden says, nodding toward my plate. "I'm sure she'll share if you ask her nicely."

As Philip and I meet each other's gaze over the top of Aiden's head, we both smile. I offer Philip my plate, and he takes one of the remaining strawberries and pops the entire thing in his mouth.

A big gray minivan pulls up to the front door, and Jake hops out and climbs the steps. "Let's go get your mom and sisters, pal."

Aiden jumps to his feet. "Excuse me, but I have to go."

Once they're back inside the house, Philip smiles as he shakes his head. "That kid."

"He's adorable," I say.

"Do you like kids?"

I nod.

Philip reaches over and steals another strawberry from my plate—one that I'd already bitten in half—and pops it into his mouth. "Delicious," he says as he licks his lips.

My face heats to a hundred degrees because I'm pretty sure he's not talking about fruit.

The door behind us opens again, and out walks Jake and

Annie and Aiden. Jake and Annie are each carrying a twin baby girl.

Philip stands to clear the way for them. He shifts to stand in front of me, blocking the sun as I gaze up at him. "It's not fair of me to ask you to wait," he says quietly so no one overhears him.

I rise to my feet, and because I'm one step up from him, we're standing eye to eye for a change. Usually, I have to crane my neck to meet his gaze. "It's not fair of me to ask *you* to wait," I say, throwing his words right back at him.

He grins like I just issued a challenge. "Oh, I'll gladly wait for you, baby. You can count on it."

I smile, feeling a whole lot more hopeful about the future. *Yeah, I'll wait for him.* I'll wait until I'm eighteen, and then no one can tell us we can't be together.

He holds out his pinky finger, and it takes me a moment to catch on. *A pinky swear.* I hook my pinky around his, and we shake.

I think we just made an oath.

When he quietly says, "Ride or die, baby," my heart does a somersault.

The front door opens again, and a whole slew of people stream out the door, including my dad and Erin, a bunch of McIntyres, and the rest of the hot guys. Looks like the party's over. Everyone's heading home.

"Time to go, Haley," Dad says as he heads across the driveway toward his SUV. He's carrying my bag, his, and Erin's.

Philip takes my plate from me. "I'll take this in for you."

I glance up at Philip once more, then head down the steps to the drive and walk toward our vehicle. Just before I climb into the back seat, I look back at Philip, who's right where I left him. He's standing there, still holding my plate. His other hand is on his hip, and he looks so freaking hot my body heats to a million degrees. His eyes are locked on me.

"Get in the vehicle, Haley," my dad says impatiently as he guns the engine. He and Erin are already belted in and ready to go.

"I'm coming."

I can't help smiling all the way back to the city. Philip said he'd wait for me, and I'll damn sure wait for him. Nothing and no one could keep me from him.

He's my ride or die, and I'm his.

30

Beth McIntyre

Everyone's gone, and the house feels so empty. It's certainly quiet. My mom got teary-eyed when we hugged goodbye out front.

"Mom, we're going to see each other again tomorrow." We're planning to go to her house for dinner tomorrow night, along with Tyler and Ian.

I hug Bridget and Calum goodbye as they load their car. I hug Shane's siblings and their significant others.

We said goodbye to Mack and Erin and Haley, to Philip and Miguel. Hannah's already gone—she left early in the morning with Liam. Killian's gone too. He left right after Hannah did.

Sam and Cooper are already packed up, and they started off for home just a few minutes ago.

We're the only ones left.

After everyone drives off, Shane and I go back inside. Elly has Ava and Luke in the kitchen with her, Luke in his high chair and Ava in her baby seat on the table.

I sit at the kitchen table. "I already miss everyone," I tell Elly. "But it's also nice when the house is quiet."

Elly nods. "Family visits are precious, but it can get to be a bit overwhelming. I wouldn't trade them for anything, but it is nice when it's just you and Shane. And now these two adorable little ones." Elly reaches down to tickle Luke's foot, making him squeal.

As he drinks milk from his sippy cup, he kicks his foot and laughs.

Ava is sound asleep.

Elly reaches out to stroke Ava's cheek. "Do you think you'll have more kids?"

I smile. "We haven't really discussed it yet, but I imagine we will. I think Shane wants a big family like his parents have. I always wanted a big family, too. So, yeah. I imagine we'll have more."

"Have more what?" Shane says as he walks into the kitchen.

"More babies," I reply. "Elly asked if we wanted more kids."

Shane stands behind my chair and leans down to kiss the top of my head and rest his hands on my shoulders. "I'd love to have more," he says, "but I think it's up to Beth."

George walks into the kitchen and stops at the sink to wash his hands. "That's everyone," he says. "Everyone has headed home." As he dries his hands on a towel, he walks over to the table and peers down at Luke and Ava. "You two sure do make pretty kids, Beth," he says in his deep voice.

Shane leaves us to go finish packing up the Escalade. Then he comes to get me and the kids, and together we buckle the kids into their car seats.

Shane hugs Elly. "Thank you for taking such good care of us."

She brushes off his words. "You don't need to thank me, dear. It's my pleasure."

"This place wouldn't be the same without you and George," Shane says.

George joins us on the front steps and shakes Shane's hand. Then he hugs me. "Come back soon," he says. "This place is mighty quiet without you kids."

I have mixed emotions as we drive away from the house. It's good to be getting home, but I always miss this place when we're not here. It's hard to be in two places at once.

Shane reaches for my hand and brings it to his lips to kiss. "You okay?"

Smiling, I nod. "Perfect."

Our drive back to the penthouse is a quiet one. Both kids fall asleep as soon as we reach the highway. I rest my hand on Shane's thigh as he drives, loving the feel of his leg muscles flexing beneath my palm.

I can't help thinking back to the first time we visited Shane's estate in Kenilworth. I was blown away by the size of the house—thinking it looked more like a lodge than a home. Everything about Shane was overwhelming to me back then—his wealth, his resources, the extent that he would go to protect me.

So much has changed since the first time we met. I've grown a lot. I feel so much stronger now emotionally. I'm more confident, thanks to running the bookstore. I finally have passion in my life now, a healthy sexual relationship, a huge extended family of amazing men and women, and now two precious children of my own. And it's all because I met Shane.

He glances over at me with a quizzical look on his face. "Everything all right?"

I nod. "Yes. I'm just thinking about all the changes in my life over the past couple of years."

He clasps my hand and kisses it. "They're good ones, I hope?"

I smile, feeling heat flush my cheeks. "Yes. Very much so."

When we arrive at our apartment building, we're greeted in the underground parking garage by Sam and Cooper. They help us carry in our luggage. Shane carries Ava's car seat, and I carry a sleepy Luke. We all ride up in the private elevator to our shared home.

"It's good to have everyone home," Cooper says as he sets our luggage on the floor just inside the penthouse. "How about I get some lunch started?"

Sam throws his arm around Cooper's shoulder and kisses his cheek. "Thank you. I'm starving."

Luke raises his head from my shoulder and says, "Eat?" in a sleepy voice.

Cooper laughs. "Yes, little man. It's time to eat."

Sam holds his hands out to Luke, and Luke goes right to him. "I'll take care of this little guy while you get the baby girl situated."

Ava's still sound asleep, so Shane carries her car seat to our bedroom. I unbuckle her and lift her out. Shane peers over my shoulder at her.

"Sleep well, little sweet pea," I tell her as I lay her in the bassinet.

Shane and I head out to the kitchen to help prepare lunch and visit with the guys. With all the goings on at Kenilworth over the weekend, we didn't get to spend much quality time with our favorite roommates.

Cooper pulls a package of steaks out of the fridge. "I think I'll fire up the grill on the roof and cook these babies."

While he's working on that, I put some potatoes in the oven to bake.

As Shane gathers ingredients to make a salad, Sam prepares a peanut butter and jelly sandwich for Luke and cuts it up into tiny bite-sized pieces.

A sense of warm contentment and well-being flows through me as I observe my family and wonder how I got so lucky.

* * *

That night, as Shane and I settle into bed, he pulls me into his arms and begins rubbing my back. Tingles and shivers cascade through my body, and I sink into his heat.

"How are you feeling?" he asks me, his lips pressed against my forehead.

"I'm feeling pretty good. Still sore, but it's getting better."

"Good. I'm glad to hear that. We'll make an appointment for you to follow up later this week with Dr. Shaw."

"And Ava has a follow-up appointment with the pediatrician this week too."

Shane's quiet for a moment, seemingly deep in thought. "It's going to be pretty hectic with two kids now. Twice the work."

I smile. "But twice the joy. Look at your folks. They raised seven kids. I now realize they're superparents."

"I was just wondering if it'll be too much to see to the needs of two kids and still manage Clancy's. Have you thought about handing the manager's job over to Erin permanently? You know she'd do a great job."

My heart starts pounding at the thought of giving up the manager's job. The bookstore means the world to me. And I love being there with Erin and Sam and Mack. "I hadn't really considered it."

"It's something for you to think about," he says. "I don't want you overstressed or overworked."

He kisses the top of my head and switches off the light.

"Goodnight, sweetheart. I love you."

"I love you, too."

Epilogue

Eight Weeks Later

Beth McIntyre

"Are you sure you're ready to go back to work?" Shane asks as I pull on a loose-fitting dress over a pair of leggings. He's standing just inside our closet, watching me get dressed. He's already dressed for work in his suit and tie. "There's no rush, sweetheart. Maybe you should take a little more time off."

I smooth my hands over the dress—and over my soft, squishy belly. I still have quite a ways to go to lose this pregnancy weight. I turn sideways to observe myself in a standing mirror. "Do I still look pregnant?"

Smiling, he comes up behind me, slips his arms around my waist, and kisses the side of my neck, sending a shiver down my spine. "You look perfect."

I laugh. "You didn't exactly answer the question." I turn and wrap my arms around his waist. "Yes, I'm ready to go back. I feel great, and I miss my bookstore. I especially miss Erin and

Mack."

"Honey, you can see Erin and Mack anytime you want. They live two floors down from us."

He's right. And I do see them pretty regularly in our building, at least a few times a week. They often come up to have dinner with us, or we go down to their apartment. But it's not the same as spending the entire day at work with Erin. "It's not the same. The three of us have a lot of fun at work." Meaning Sam, Erin, and I.

Shane follows me out of the closet just as Cooper walks into our suite carrying Luke, who's dressed and chewing on a piece of buttered toast. Ava is currently asleep in her bassinet, which stands at the foot of our bed. I've got their diaper bag packed, and at this very moment, Sam is carrying it downstairs to the Escalade.

I'm blessed to have a nursery attached to my office at the bookstore. Lindsey is our full-time nanny who will help me take care of the kids while I manage the store.

"The little man's ready to go," Cooper says as he wipes Luke's mouth with a napkin. "He's had breakfast, and I just changed his diaper."

"Everything's ready," I tell Shane. I go up on my toes to kiss him. "Don't worry." I pat his firm chest reassuringly. "Everything will be fine."

He's been away from the office on paternity leave for the past two months, spending his time at home with me and the kids. I know it's hard to go back to our normal work routine. I think he's struggling with the idea more than he expected.

"Call me if there are any issues," he says reluctantly. "If you're feeling unwell, or if—"

Sam walks into our bedroom. "Joe's here." He takes Luke from Cooper. "I'll carry the boy. You get the little princess."

I've hardly seen Joe Rucker, my driver, since I've been on maternity leave. We have a lot of catching up to do.

"I'll call you if there's any problem," I tell Shane, hoping to placate him. "I promise."

Despite the frown on his handsome face, he nods. He's not happy about the idea, but at least he respects my wish to return to work.

"Fine," he says. Then he looks to Sam, my full-time bodyguard and best friend. "Don't let her overdo it."

With a grin, Sam salutes Shane. "Copy that, boss." Sam winks at me as if he and I are in cahoots with each other, when we're both just placating Shane. *Get ready to party*, he mouths to me.

Shane gives Sam a droll look that clearly proves he's onto us.

We all head down to the garage. Joe is standing next to the Escalade, a big smile on his handsome face.

"Hey, big guy," Sam says as he high-fives the six-foot-tall African-American former heavyweight boxer who's built like a tank.

"Hello, Sam. Hello, Beth." Joe gives me a gentle hug. He ruffles Luke's hair and peeks in on Ava, who's cooing in her car seat. "That is one mighty pretty baby," he says.

As we pull away, I glance back at Shane. He and Cooper are

standing beside Shane's vintage silver Jaguar, watching us exit the parking garage.

Sam reaches back from the front passenger seat and pats my leg. "Don't worry. He's a big boy. He'll be fine."

I laugh. But I understand what Shane's feeling. We've both been home with the kids since Ava was born, and it's a bit unsettling to finally go back to our normal routine.

Luke's in his car seat playing with his favorite stuffed kitty, jabbering to himself. Ava's content in her car seat. The rocking motion of a vehicle always soothes her.

"It's good to be back, isn't it?" Joe asks in his deep baritone voice.

Relaxing in my seat, I nod. "It is."

When we arrive at Clancy's, Joe pulls up to the sidewalk outside the front doors. Sam helps me climb out of the vehicle. He releases Luke from his car seat, and I unfasten Ava's car seat. Mack and Erin are both waiting for us at the entrance.

"Oh, my god, you're back," Erin cries as she runs out onto the sidewalk to hug me. After she hugs Sam, she holds her arms out to Luke, and he lunges into her embrace. "Hello, sweetie." As she kisses his cheek, he wraps his little arms around her neck and squeezes. "I've missed you so much."

"Welcome back," Mack says as he holds the doors for us.

Sam takes Ava's car seat from me and carries her inside. There's a small crowd of employees waiting to greet us, including Lindsey. It's her first day back to work, too, as I gave her two months of paid time off while I was on maternity leave.

I say hello to everyone. Naturally, they all want a peek at Ava, who's still sound asleep in her car seat.

While Sam and Lindsey take the kids upstairs to the nursery, which is in the administrative wing, Erin walks me around the store, pointing out new displays, new releases, and the new fall merchandise. It's hard to believe that it's November already, and Thanksgiving is just around the corner. Everything looks absolutely perfect—as I knew it would. Erin's a fantastic assistant manager.

I don't miss the fact that Mack is following us around the store. His gaze never wanders far from Erin. I need to get her upstairs to my office so we can dish about Mack and how things are going between them.

When we eventually make it up to my office on the second floor, I peek in at the kids. Lindsey's seated in a rocking chair with Luke on her lap. She's holding a child's board book in her hands, and Luke is cuddling a stuffed elephant.

"I took him to the children's section to let him pick out a book," she says, nodding to the elephant. "He picked that out instead. You should have seen the way his eyes lit up when he saw it, Beth," Lindsey says, grinning guiltily. "I didn't have the heart to tell him no. I hope it's okay."

"It's fine."

Luke holds the elephant up to me and grins.

I check on Ava, who's sleeping in one of the two cribs. "Let me know when she wakes up," I tell Lindsey. "She'll be hungry."

"Will do."

When I return to my office, I find Erin and Sam seated on the sofa in front of the big picture window overlooking North Michigan Avenue. That sure is a sight for sore eyes. I've missed this so much, just hanging with them.

Sam puts his arm around Erin's shoulders and draws her close. I know he's missed this too. "So, come on. Tell us how it's going," Sam says. "Tell us *everything*."

Erin grins. "Are you asking about the store or about my personal life?"

"Both," he says. "But mostly about your personal life. Spill the tea, sister. How's the big guy treating you?"

"Mack's great," she says, her dimples appearing as she smiles. "Everything's going really well."

Sam laughs. "We need details, girl," he says, winking at me.

"You know he loves to tease you," I tell Erin.

While those two are catching up, I boot up my computer and start the daunting process of wading through two months of unread e-mails. Despite my overflowing inbox, it feels good to be back at work.

After making a valiant dent in my backlog of e-mails, I take a break so I can peek in at Luke and Ava. Luke and Lindsey are seated on the rug, playing with Luke's new stuffed elephant toy. Ava is just starting to stir in her crib.

Not surprisingly, Shane calls me mid-morning to see how things are going. "Everything's fine," I tell him. "Ava has slept most of the morning. Luke's having fun playing with Lindsey. I think he missed her. How is your day going?"

"It's fine," he says. "Truthfully, it's been a bit boring. I've been reading through a stack of case reports all morning, trying to play catch-up. The reason I called is because I miss you. I miss seeing your face and hearing your voice. And I miss the kids."

"We miss you, too."

* * *

When I leave the nursery, I find Sam seated alone on the sofa, playing a game on his phone. "Where's Erin?"

He nods toward the door. "She went downstairs. Said she needed to get back to work."

I sit at my desk and resume wading through my backlog of e-mails until something catches my ear—a loud, belligerent voice that sounds like it's coming from downstairs.

I meet Sam's gaze. "Did you hear that?"

Nodding, he shoots to his feet and opens my office door to listen. We hear a man shouting at someone.

"What in the world?" I say as I jump out of my chair.

"Stay here," Sam says as he bolts out the door.

I follow him. Once we're out of the administrative wing and on the upstairs sales floor, we can hear the irate man more clearly. I peer over the wrought-iron railing at the customer service desk down below on the main floor. Erin is standing behind the counter, with Mack planted firmly at her side. Across the counter from her is a pissed-off customer.

Oh, no. No way.

"What the fuck do I have to do to get decent service around here?" the man shouts at Erin.

"Oh, hell no," Sam mutters as he takes off down the stairs. He glances back at me. "Wait in your office."

I am not staying back and hiding in my office while he and Mack deal with this guy. I'm right behind him.

A small crowd of curious onlookers has already gathered around the customer service desk.

The irate customer, an elderly man wearing baggy gray trousers and an oversized red plaid jacket, is practically screaming at Erin. "I ordered that book over a month ago!" he yells. "Why isn't it in yet? What's wrong with you people?"

Erin is pale as can be, but she keeps her calm. "Sir, I'm sorry, but your book is on backorder with our distributor. As soon as it's back in stock, they'll send it to us. We'll call you—"

The man slams his fist on the counter. "That's bullshit. You probably forgot to order it, didn't you? Well, hell. I might as well go somewhere else."

Erin shows him an order sheet. While her hand is visibly shaking, she doesn't falter. "We did order the book five weeks ago, but as I said, it's on backorder. The publisher is behind schedule—"

Sam takes a step closer, preparing to intervene. Mack is standing right beside Erin, his arms crossed over his impressive chest as he glares at the customer.

"You're incompetent," the man sneers, making Erin wince.

"Get the manager. I want to speak to the manager, now."

As I take a step forward, Sam catches my eye and shakes his head. "Let us handle this."

"That's enough!" I say as I approach the man. "You can't talk to my employees like that."

The man looks dismissively at me. "I want to speak to the manager. Right now!"

"You are speaking to her," I say. "I'm the manager."

He scowls. "You are? Please. Who's really in charge here?"

Fed up with this jackass, I look to Mack. In a calm, measured voice, I say, "Would you please escort this gentleman out of my bookstore?"

"Gladly," he says.

"You can't do that!" the man yells as Mack comes around the counter and takes hold of his arm.

"Oh, yes I can," Mack says as he hauls the man toward the front doors. "You heard the lady."

I walk around to the other side of the counter and put my arm around Erin's shoulders. She's shaking, but she has a determined look on her face. She shows me the copy of the order form. "I did order the book, five weeks ago. The publisher is behind on printing."

"Of course you did," I say as I give her shoulders a squeeze. Then I lean close so no customers can overhear me and whisper, "He's an asshole."

As Erin laughs, the tension leaves her body.

The customers standing around watching the debacle start

to drift away. Sam comes up to the counter and reaches across it to take Erin's hands in his. "You were awesome."

Erin smiles.

Then Sam looks at me. "And you were magnificent. I love seeing you all riled up and acting like a mama bear."

"No one yells at Erin like that," I say. "No one yells at any of my employees."

Mack rejoins us. "I told him he's banned from the store. He can find his damn book somewhere else."

"Fine with me," I say.

Erin's color has returned to her cheeks, and she looks pretty darn proud of herself. I'm proud of her too.

"I've missed this so much, you guys," I say, leaning my head against Erin's. "It feels so good to be back."

"I think this calls for a coffee break," Sam says as he nods toward the in-house café. "Come on. I'm buying."

* * *

The kids and I, along with Sam, make it back to the penthouse just a few minutes before Shane returns from his office at McIntyre Security.

Sam and I are seated on one of the sofas in the great room, and Ava's sleeping in my arms after a marathon nursing session. I think she's going to have as big an appetite as her brother.

Luke's sitting on the rug at our feet playing with his toys.

When we hear the elevator doors chime, Luke climbs to his feet. He's learned what that sound means. Someone's home. He rushes toward the foyer door. "Dada!"

Shane walks through the door and scoops Luke up into his arms. "Hey, buddy." He kisses Luke's cheek.

It's a bit of a shock seeing Shane in his customary charcoal gray suit and white shirt. He looks so handsome, just like he did the day we met.

"Hi, sweetheart," he says as we meet halfway for a kiss. He bends down and kisses Ava's forehead. "How'd she do today?"

"She was an angel," I say.

When Luke starts squirming impatiently, Shane sets him down and takes Ava from me. "How'd your first day go?"

"She kicked ass," Sam says from the kitchen as he refills his water bottle and takes a long gulp. "We had an irate customer in the store today, yelling his fool head off at poor Erin, and Beth put the jackass in his place. She had Mack throw him out of the store."

Shane looks to me. "Is that so?"

I smile. "It was very cathartic. I won't tolerate anyone yelling at my employees that way."

"Good job," Shane says as he wraps his free arm around me and pulls me close. "The most important job of a manager is to look out for her employees."

Luke returns, carrying his new stuffed elephant, which he insisted on bringing home. He holds the toy up to Shane and jabbers something unintelligible.

Shane hands me Ava so he can pick up Luke and admire his new acquisition.

Luke rests his head on Shane's shoulder and says, "Eat."

The elevator chimes once more and Cooper comes through the door.

"Hoop!" Luke says, squirming in Shane's hold.

Shane puts Luke down, and our son rushes off to see Cooper.

Cooper's holding a sack from the grocery store. "I bought burgers to grill tonight," he says. "I thought we should celebrate you two going back to work."

* * *

After a wonderful meal up on the roof and an evening spent in front of the fireplace, chatting with our closest friends and laughing over Luke's antics, my eyes are so heavy I can hardly keep them open.

"Bedtime," Shane says as he picks up Luke. "I'll get him ready for bed," he says to me. "You get Ava ready."

Once both kids are tucked into their respective beds, Shane and I rendezvous in our private suite.

He turns the lights down low, puts on some quiet blues music, and pours himself a shot of whiskey. I opt for a Coke instead. No alcohol for me right now.

The suit came off a long time earlier. Now he's wearing a pair of gray sweats that ride low on his hips. He removes his T-shirt and sits back on the sofa in our private little sitting area.

I disappear into the bathroom and change into a sheer, silky nightgown that barely covers my ass. And I mean *barely*. I'm also not wearing any panties.

I had a check-up yesterday with my obstetrician, and she gave me the green light to resume regular activities. And that means sex is back on the table.

It's been two long months.

I join Shane on the sofa, sitting sideways so I can lay my legs over his lap. He skims a hand up my leg, over my thigh, and keeps going until it disappears beneath the hem of my nightie.

I've been waiting for this night for a whole week now, and I'm ready to enjoy it.

"You forgot your panties," he observes, the corners of his lips rising in a grin.

"Oh, I didn't forget." My pulse is racing in anticipation. I just want him to *touch* me.

But to my disappointment, he doesn't. His hand meanders back down my leg to caress my ankle.

"Would you like a foot massage?" he asks as he takes one of my feet in his hands. He begins kneading my sole.

"Um." *How do I say this politely?*

No, I want you to fuck me?

I think if I used that word right now, he'd flip. In a good way.

"A foot massage isn't exactly what I had in mind," I say.

His eyebrow arches. "Really?"

"Yeah, really." I pull my foot from his grasp and run it along the length of his very large erection. "I was thinking of something else."

His expressions tightens and he swallows hard. His chest rises with a strong, deep breath, and I realize he's holding back.

He's worried about hurting me.

"Shane?"

His nostrils flare. "Hmm?"

"Dr. Shaw said it's fine."

His bright blue gaze meets mine. "I know, but—"

"No buts." I stand, slip off my nightgown, and move in front of him, naked.

His heated gaze methodically skims my body from head to toe with a hunger that steals my breath. "Are you trying to kill me?"

I laugh. "No. That would defeat the purpose."

He grins. "And what's the purpose?"

"You fucking me."

His eyes widen, as I knew they would. He's not used to hearing me talk like that. Shane shoots to his feet and shucks his sweats off, leaving himself naked too. His erection is thick, lifting in the air as it defies gravity.

"You're playing with fire, sweetheart," he says, his voice a low growl. "It's been a very long time."

"Tell me about it," I say as I run my index finger down the center of his chest and to his erection. I wrap my fingers around him and squeeze, relishing in the heat of him as he throbs in my grip.

Without warning, he bends and scoops me into a fireman's hold. I shriek in surprise as he carries me across our room to the bed. He lays me on the bed and gazes down at me, his expression fierce. "I will try my best to be gentle this first time," he says.

I reach for him and pull him down onto me. "I don't want gentle. I want *you*."

When he finally gets around to sliding into me, after seeing to my pleasure first, he is gentle, and so attentive that my heart swells with emotion.

This man is my *everything*.

And we are *his*.

* * *

Thank you so much for reading *Special Delivery!* I hope you enjoyed this installment in the McIntyre Security Bodyguard Series. Stay tuned for news about more books in this series.

My next release is *Search and Rescue*, which is Hannah McIntyre and Killian Devereaux's thrilling romance that takes place in a small mountain town in the Rocky Mountains. This is the first book in my spin-off series called "McIntyre Search and Rescue."

* * *

If you'd like to sign up for my newsletter, download my free short stories, or locate my contact information, visit my website: www.aprilwilsonauthor.com

* * *

For links to my growing list of audiobooks and upcoming releases, visit my website: www.aprilwilsonauthor.com

* * *

I interact daily with readers in my Facebook reader group (Author April Wilson's Reader Group) where I post frequent updates and share weekly teasers for upcoming releases. Come join me!

Books by April Wilson

McIntyre Security Bodyguard Series:
Vulnerable
Fearless
Shane (a novella)
Broken
Shattered
Imperfect
Ruined
Hostage
Redeemed
Marry Me (a novella)
Snowbound (a novella)
Regret
With This Ring (a novella)
Collateral Damage
Special Delivery

McIntyre Security Search and Rescue Series:
Search and Rescue

A Tyler Jamison Novel:
Somebody to Love
Somebody to Hold

A British Billionaire Romance:
Charmed (co-written with Laura Riley)

Audiobooks and Upcoming Releases:
For links to my audiobooks and upcoming releases, visit my website:
www.aprilwilsonauthor.com

Printed in Great Britain
by Amazon